GERTRUDE OF DENMARK

BY THE SAME AUTHOR

"''She looks like the Holy Mother,' said the King''"

GERTRUDE OF DENMARK

AN INTERPRETATIVE ROMANCE

BY
LILLIE BUFFUM CHACE WYMAN

INTRODUCTION BY
COURTNEY LANGDON

WILDSIDE PRESS

THE PLIMPTON PRESS · NORWOOD · MASSACHUSETTS
PRINTED IN THE UNITED STATES OF AMERICA

DEDICATORY PREFACE

I CAN think of no better introducing words for this rather bizarre effort at interpretation than those which were once spoken to me by Ellen Terry, "Oh, didn't Shakspeare know a lot about us women!"

I wish, however, in addition, to thank certain friends of mine for the encouragement they gave me to write out in this romantic form my seriously held theories. Their names are linked together in a circlet of golden recollections within my mind. They are (dispensing with all social titles) Courtney Langdon, Susan T. Langdon, Anne C. Chace, Margaret W. Morley, and Demetra Vaka Kenneth-Brown.

But the book itself is, from inner necessity, dedicated to the memory of John Crawford Wyman.

INTRODUCTION

THOSE who read and study Mrs. Wyman's Romance will not be disappointed, whether they look for an original and intuitive study of those ever engaging phases of human nature—motherhood and girlhood; or, on the other hand, look for an original bit of Shakspearean criticism applied to the elusive problem of Hamlet's character. For the former, I can predict nothing but wondering praise and absorbing interest; for the latter, such interest as is bound to be aroused, when settled opinions are squarely challenged, and when orthodox notions are put again upon the defensive.

As an interpretation of "Hamlet," this Romance by a greatly gifted woman and writer must necessarily run the gauntlet of adverse criticism from those who hold any of the several conflicting interpretations already in possession of this "parlous" field. It happens that Mrs. Wyman's conception of "Hamlet" as a play, and of its leading characters, notably of Hamlet himself, is not that which, rightly or wrongly, I am led by the play itself to support; that, however, is a matter of little relative consequence. But even if Mrs. Wyman's view should win its way to acceptance, therein would not lie the greatest outstanding merit of her work. Out of a few suggestions afforded by the text of "Hamlet," she has built up by dint of intuitive and sympathetic imagination what she has herself called "a romance," based upon

Introduction

the character of the motherhood of one, who was, and upon the maidenhood of another, who might have been, "the imperial jointress" of a warlike state. Under the pleasing veil of supernatural confidences, she has seen in her "mind's eye" the girlhood of Hamlet's mother, and that of his "fair Ophelia," in such an interesting way, that the reader, as he reads, will care little whether Shakspeare so understood them or not; but will be absorbed in the book's revelation of how its author understood woman's nature. Incidentally, the progressive criticism of the play's text will be found dotted with flashes of insight, which cannot fail to be gratefully accepted by readers and scholars alike.

Believing as I do that spiritual and moral insight must "in the world's allowance o'erweigh a whole theatre" of merely intellectual criticism, I am confident that my own merely intellectual dissent with the interpretation will serve only to enhance whatever value may be attached to my enthusiastic approval of the concentrated life-experience, thought and feeling revealed in the remarkable Romance, with which that criticism is fused. In short, while I do not think that Shakspeare conceived Mrs. Wyman's "Gertrude of Denmark," I do feel that, had he done so, and had he given her conception of the character dramatic form, it would have ranked high among his tragedies, as one of the greatest revelations of what is in woman.

CourtNey Langdon

Brown University
[viii]

GERTRUDE OF DENMARK

GERTRUDE OF DENMARK

PROLOGUE

WAS it in a dream or a reverie that Gertrude of Denmark came and begged me to tell her story to the world? I was lying on a lounge which stretched along in front of two windows. There was a third window, in the wall close behind my head. Old pine trees stood outside, near the corner of the house whose foundations were laid on a little higher ground than that in which they had been rooted for an unknown number of centuries; and because of this lay of the land, their branches inclosed that triangle of my room and extended their evergreen arms across the window panes.

I was drowsily holding, but not reading, a volume of Shakspeare when she came. She looked to be a woman forty-six or seven years old, with the softest brown eyes you ever saw, that kind of pale clear complexion which, being neither brunette nor blonde, has no need of any flush to make it beautiful . . .

features having much daintiness of form, a perfect mouth, indefinable charm and grace everywhere;—such was she. Her hair was of an amber-tinted brown, and it waved and clustered around her head, while a few curls dropped down, as if they themselves wanted to touch her neck.

She spoke to me in English, and when I questioned her about her knowledge of that language, she answered "Oh, after Shakspeare wrote in England, many wise ones, in our 'undiscovered country', came to the opinion that his language should be used there. And naturally I, whose story he had told, joined that party and learned it. But it has made my heart ache sorely to read what he wrote about me and take note of what he did not say in my behoof."

Then she began to plead with me, "Will you tell that story of mine over again," she implored. "Hamlet wanted Horatio to live on in order to report him and his 'cause aright.' I had no chance, before I died, to ask anybody to protect me from the writers, the critics,—and the actresses!"

After a pause, she asked, "Did you never wonder why Shakspeare brought Hecuba into his play?" "Yes," I said, and she answered, "Hecuba was a mother;—and I also was a mother."

Gertrude of Denmark

After that, for many weeks and occasionally for years Gertrude kept coming to me. (Was it in dream or in reverie?) As she talked, I often fell a-wondering why Shakspeare, who could do all things, had chosen to veil this woman's soul in the mists of his clouded tragedy. Perhaps he thought that the mother of a mysterious being should be herself fashioned out of mystery.

Yet, however he may obscure character and motive, it is not in accord with Shakspeare's usual method to leave uncertain the physical connection of his personages with a sin or crime which closely concerns them. Gertrude is frankly accused in the play of incest and inferentially of adultery. Yet she is nowhere shown as quite confessing to adultery, or as uttering a seriously unworthy speech or as performing a base action. The worst, that need be inferred from her own words, may well be held as an admission that she was sometimes disturbed by the fear that marriage with a first husband's brother was sinful in its very nature,—an ethical question much mooted in Shakspeare's England.

I said to her once, "Of course Shakspeare wrote out your story in the terms of England's moral code."

"Yes," she sighed, "that great Englishman was a wizard, and he knew all past events and the speech thereof, as though all had been written down in a book for him to read and copy. And though what we said in Danish he wrote out in the verse of another tongue, he did report our deeds and our sayings very nearly as we did the deeds and spoke the words. But he left out some record of our thoughts and omitted to tell some things that would have revealed me more truly than I am shown in his pages. I do not know why he thus blurred the outlines of my real self unless it were because of the English antipathy to the marriage of a man with his brother's widow."

I easily discovered that Gertrude was not a profound thinker nor a very wise judge of the motives which actuated people around her. Yet not commonplace was the personality of this woman, whom a great king had loved and trusted all his life, and as a ghost still loved with tender compassion even while, like a man, he suspected and reviled her,— this woman to whom a villain clung with desperate affection, and to whom Ophelia gave blossoms.

I also soon learned that either Gertrude did not know history, or that one of the inhibitions, placed upon ghostly intercourse with fleshly folk, related to speech upon such topics, as to whether her son Hamlet had actually attended a university in Wittenberg several hundred years before there was any university in that place. She grew faint in color and diaphanous in texture, before my very eyes, or she vanished completely, if ·I sought her help to straighten out things pertaining to chronology and synchronology.

Once I asked her whether the elder Hamlet had seemed to be a much better man than Claudius was, before the latter had dabbled in absolute criminality, basing my inquiry on the ghost's own admission that he had committed "foul crimes." She contracted her brows a little, and her eyes became wistful; then she said, "Both kings let me see them only when they were comporting themselves virtuously, and each had a regal bearing—but King Hamlet's demeanor was the grander and he was very handsome. Claudius was not."

Once she said thoughtfully, "You wonder that I cannot answer all the questions you ask. Well, Shakspeare was a wizard on earth, but we others were not that when we lived in the flesh; coming and dwelling here as spirits does indeed give us the opportunity to learn some things of which we were ignorant before. But it does not make us, like him, know and understand everything pertaining to human life."

To another question she answered, "No, I have never seen the Great Wizard himself, I fain would meet him and plead my cause direct to him. I am told that he consorts mainly with Bacon, though for the last century he has been much with Macbeth and his Lady and with young Romeo and Juliet."

I ceased effort at critical investigation and merely studied the ghostly woman herself. She related incidents over and over, till I had got them by heart, and she told everything in such dramatic fashion that I knew how she had looked and moved at every moment of which she spoke, and I even grew, now and then, to feel better able to interpret her analytically than she herself could do it.

We read the play together, going carefully over the scenes in which she does not appear. Of these portions of the drama, she told me much of what she had in some way heard, and gave her own thought about the happenings in them. In consequence of all this study and talk I grew to feel competent to make the connected narrative which I now endeavor to present to the consideration of any one who may care to read the story of a Queen Mother.

CHAPTER I

GERTRUDE was a girl of princely rank, born on the continent, motherless from infancy (like most of Shakspeare's heroines) and brought up, as was fitting, in a convent. She saw her father only two or three times after she was old enough to remember the sight. She knew that she had a brother, but she had no recollection of ever having seen him, when, being herself twelve years old, she was told that he had been killed "in the wars." She knew nothing of the world, of ceremony or of action, when, the day that she was fifteen, she was wedded in the morning to a regal stranger, just twice her age, whom she had first seen two days previously. She was, however, glad enough to marry him. He impressed her imagination by his stateliness, and he touched her heart by his playful, half paternal, half lover-like manner. Marriage was also welcome, because it procured her release from the convent, for Gertrude, though good and docile, was not a religious enthusiast. She had sometimes yawned over her beads.

Married and placed in her palace, she was happy and her affection grew steadily for the man who was so loving to her, "That he might not beteem the winds of Heaven visit her face too roughly."

The King had a brother (as all the world now knows) named Claudius. At the time of Gertrude's marriage, he was about twenty years old,—a clumsy low-statured boy who often showed her much awkward, kindly attention. She played games with him. She learned all his little ways, graciously submitted to some, and soothed in him and in his brother the irritation which others of them were apt to produce.

She once said to me: "I used to feel that Claudius, when he was young, was not at ease with life because he had not been born with quite the right disposition. I thought that he was trying to hammer one out for himself. I wanted to help him."

She did not love Claudius, except in ordinary sisterly fashion, and she never troubled herself to think whether or not he were in love with her. She knew very well, before she had been married six months, that she loved the King; yet it is possible that her love was never quite of the spontaneous and ardent variety. That did not matter, for Gertrude considered marriage, from whatever motive contracted, to be a sacrament. Marriage, spiritually speaking, was the object of her religion.

As the years passed, Claudius was away a great deal for purposes of war, of hunting and diplomacy.

Once she became aware that there was bad blood between the brothers, but she did not learn what had caused it, and the ill-feeling seemed to pass. Her thought about it was simple, namely, that the King, of course, was right, and that Claudius was very foolish. So to help make things pleasant, she worked lace cuffs for Claudius, and smiled at the King, and told him how the baby Hamlet's eyes shone big and mystical when he stammered out his prayers.

At another time she heard Claudius say rather angrily to his brother, "Ask Gertrude what she thinks; she is far wiser than you about such, and a great many other matters, too!" They were all three in the garden, but the men were at a little distance from her and behind some shrubbery. King Hamlet's loud laughter came to her ears but she did not hear his words in answer, and as the little Hamlet just then started to run from her down the blossom-bordered pathway, she ran after him with a gay smile on her lips.

She never asked either man in what ways did Claudius deem her to be so wise.

Motherhood brought to Gertrude her fullest development. She was not quite sixteen when Hamlet was born. She became a Madonna at once. There were two or three children afterwards, but not one of them lived many hours. She had not quite come out of her gulf of maternal pain, before each of those children had turned itself into the memory of a thwarted hope. It was Hamlet therefore always with her—Hamlet first and last and all the time.

Clad in a dull blue gown, faintly bespangled, she often sat in a high-backed chair made of carved wood inlaid with gold and jewels, and sitting there, she would hold her child on her knees. One afternoon the two brothers, standing nearby, saw her thus.

"She looks like the Holy Mother," said the King. "I think that I will give her to the church here to take the place of their wooden image of the Mother."

"She is the most sacred creature on earth," answered Claudius, as he whirled on his heels and walked away. The King came nearer, yet not very near, to Gertrude, sat down, told her of the little colloquy and then declared that he was jealous of her love for "that baby."

She gazed at him wonderingly, went across the room, kissed him, returned, took up the child and bent low over it so as to hide her face. After a while, the King laughed, and departed for the hunt.

During all the ensuing years, Claudius, staring at the mother and boy, sometimes felt that her love for her son was a boon to himself, since it had, as he believed, become her intensest passion, and so had prevented her husband from being the object thereof. In those moments, he almost loved the child. At other times, he hated it, since its existence made him realize the more how far from the centre of Gertrude's life was his own abiding place.

Claudius's passion for her had its natural ups and downs, and interludes, and some of those interludes were vile, and some were of indifference, while others were almost those of holy enthusiasm. He was also ambitious, and had the kind of self-love which makes a man at once brave and cowardly. Hatred played nearly as large a part as love in the drama of his onward progress towards criminality. All these various forces, after a temporary lapse of energy in some of them, arose like giants, when he was fifty years old, and contended for the mastery of his career. Therefore it was that he, having lately returned from an expedition to the North Sea Islands, stole into the private gardens, and committed the deed which entailed upon him the "primal eldest curse" from Heaven.

Ceremony followed ceremony, and pageants of woe interrupted pageants of politics. Immediately after his election to the throne, Claudius demanded an audience with Gertrude. White and haggard of aspect, he flung himself upon his knees. She bade him rise up, saying it was not seemly for one, who was now a monarch, to kneel to a woman who was but the widow of greatness. He begged her forgiveness for having been chosen instead of her son to be the King of Denmark. She smiled faintly and said that all loyal people must abide by the choice of the electorate. "I pledge allegiance to your Majesty," she added and quietly asked permission to leave him.

When alone, Gertrude tried to face the situation—that is, so far as she knew what the situation was. She went to the narrow window, in her stone-walled room, and looked upon a moon-lit scene. Everything showed pallid in that light,—stone turrets, stone battlements and stone stretches inclosing stone.

She remembered that for thirty years, she had never strolled alone on a country lane. She had ridden through fields, at times, when she had most reluctantly accompanied a hunting party. She was afraid of horses, and falconry had no charms for her, but she would have liked to wander on foot among wild flowers and beside the shimmering waters of

sunlit ponds. She had sometimes seen a deep brook
near the castle. She had been borne past it in a
litter, or had galloped, with inward terror, over the
pathway under the willows on its shores.

With curious inconsequence, she thought of this
stream now when she was trying to think about Claudius and her son.

She remembered that she had once begged King
Hamlet to let her dismount and wait under the trees
until the hunt was ʻover. There were bandits drift-
ing through the country then, and he had been afraid
to leave her there even with an armed guard. She
had smiled an adoring gratitude for his timidity on
her behalf, and had ridden on.

Remembering that hour, the widowed "Majesty
of Denmark" turned drearily from the window and
gave herself up to misery.

A few days later, she tried again to think out the
facts as to what had happened, and what was likely
to happen. The question of her son's future erected
itself like a dense substance before the eyes of her
soul. Still she kept murmuring, "Before I can think
what he must do, I must decide what I can do."

She knew herself to be fitted for only one sort of
existence. She had been a queen for thirty years.
She did not know how to be anything but a queen

with a prince for a son,—both of them upheld in
their station by a king. Her soft spirit felt bruised
by the idea of being any other kind of a personage,
—bruised, as though the idea itself were a cloud of
dust beating against her face. She had been
propped, surrounded, "cabined, cribbed, confined"
indeed, but still sheltered, controlled and guided by a
settled routine of royal custom. Before she became
a royal wife she had dwelt in a secluded convent.
She had learned how to live that life and she hated
it,—hated it now in retrospect even more than when
it had been present to her—hated it as a complaisant
person will hate once or twice, though only once or
twice in a life time.

This very day Polonius had hinted to her that the
position of an abbess would be most seemly for a
widowed queen, and he had told her also that word
had come from "Old Norway," commending sanctuary as the proper retreat for such mingled nobility
and bereavement as hers.

Moreover, Hamlet, her Hamlet, had announced
his determination to return to Wittenberg and had
added that his mind would be much at ease if he
could leave her in the safe custody of the Church.
As he finished his speech, Gertrude had a sudden
vision of moments in his childhood when, tired of

play, he had been wont to come and back up in speechless confidence against her knees, certain that she would lift him to her lap. She had always lifted him. She remembered just how soft his little body had felt, and how he had been wont to gaze at her and then lay his head on her shoulder.

Now, alone in her chamber, she said to herself that there would be for her no more joy, even in motherhood, if he were in Wittenberg and she in a convent. She had lost her place. He had lost the throne. Denmark had loved him, as she did, but Denmark had weighed him in the balance and found him wanting in the qualities which its monarch should possess. Thus she saw the situation. She looked around the room and, to her excited fancy, it seemed growing narrow, its walls approaching each other, taking on the semblance of a convent cell.

A court lady came in, an aunt of Ophelia's, and, in deferential phrases, told Gertrude that speculation was busy in the palace as to whom the new king would marry, for marry now and speedily he must. "Yes," said Gertrude, "if he would have a grown son before his own death."

"Yes, madam," echoed the lady.

"A son, trained in camps and not in schools, to be elected as king," thought Gertrude.

The lady mentioned three young princesses, of whom everybody spoke in connection with the possible marriage of Claudius. "Yes, there are many princesses for a king to choose among," said Gertrude.

Then the lady said she would be loathe to serve another mistress, there in Elsinore,—and where, she asked, would the lovely dowager go when another queen should come.

An old woman tottered in and tremblingly begged her dear Majesty to use her influence, should there be a new queen, so that she herself might be retained on the nursery staff, to direct the other servants how to care for any new royal infant.

A kindly pity arose in Gertrude's heart amid the anguish that almost filled it. She laid her royal hand on the old crone's shoulder, as she answered. "All in due time, Goody. I remember thou didst mind young Lord Hamlet well."

Then, since at this moment they two were alone, they suddenly became just two women and sobbed together.

For ten days after this, Gertrude spoke no word which was not absolutely necessary.

Hamlet made no effort to see her during this period. Later she was told things which I, on hearing them, interpreted to signify that he felt wrapped around with spiritual glory because he had a mother who was going insane on account of his father's death.

Afterwards I became uncertain whether such were the feelings which had prompted Hamlet to make these utterances. So I have relegated them to that region of unsolved mystery in his being, concerning which conjecture has often been utterly futile, and I do not repeat them here.

Gertrude learned that on the eleventh day, an attendant told him that she had broken her silence, so far as to hum an old ballad. He had recognized the words, when repeated to him. He had loved that song, in evenings, when she had sung it till he slept. He softly sang it himself now, "Why, let the strucken deer go weep." Then he wrote a letter which began "To the celestial and my soul's idol, the most beautified Ophelia."

He left Elsinore that day, to visit a monastery at some distance and inspect some manuscripts there. He had sent a farewell message to his mother, who, from the window, watched him and cried as he rode away.

Gertrude awoke from her stupor of agony, to such a degree that her ladies began again to whisper in her presence, or to talk directly to her, and make surmises concerning the future as well as lamentations for the past. One spoke of a strong sanctuary near Elsinore, where the late King's grandmother had lived a guarded life and made a pious death, after fifty years of royal widowhood in a convent. Another suggested deftly that, although "Old Norway" was so decrepit, it might be well for this lovely dowager to wed his widowed state—in due time, of course; and she added that, for her part, she should be sorry to see King Claudius (the Saints preserve him) set a young wife beside him on the throne,— yet,—oh, yes—yes, she supposed that every Dane ought to rejoice were a new prince added to the royal house. Thus the gad-flies kept stinging this Danish Io, till little Ophelia cried shame upon them, whereat they vowed that they meant no harm.

After that Gertrude shut herself up in her closet and said, "No son of Claudius shall ever sit in my Hamlet's place."

Then she shuddered, fell on her knees, caught at her beads, and assured Heaven that she had not meant what her words had seemed to imply. No, no, she would never murder a baby! Or had she meant for one wicked moment, that she would do such a thing to keep her Hamlet the foremost prince of the blood? Had she meant it? For, in very truth, she had seemed to see herself with a fell intent, stealthily approaching an unguarded infant. It was only that false image of oneself, which a delirious fancy will sometimes present when the brain is reeling in the access of tormented sensation. But the horrible vision had rushed across the field of her mind's eye. She grovelled on the floor and cried.

After a while, she arose, took from a cupboard a toy with which Hamlet had played in his childhood. She kissed it. She stared around the room, then walked steadily to one of its walls, pushed aside the curtain cover and kissed the bare stone.

She had scarcely turned from that stone when the message was brought to her that the King begged for an interview, "begged" said the lady messenger, "not commanded it."

Her brain was still whirling. She did not know whether or not her body swayed. She thought for one second that "His Majesty" who was asking audience of her, was her husband,—Hamlet's father.

Then, remembering, she pressed her hands to her eyes, dropped them, glanced at her gown, lifted her head high, and, with the walk that would have betrayed a goddess, entered the outer chamber and came into the presence of Claudius. She had not seen him, except in necessary ceremony, since the hour when he had knelt before her after his election to the throne.

Now it was she who knelt. For the first time in her life, his touch was hasty and almost rough, as he raised her to her feet. She confronted him with a half smile which recognized, but condoned, his impetuosity. They were entirely alone.

"Gertrude," he said, "*marry* me! The people who loved my brother best will see, in such a marriage, a plain augury of my future policy. You and I will front the world, clothed in double dignity. The nobles elected me king. Through your clasp of my hand, my brother will bestow his blessing. Fortinbras will find no party in Denmark to help him tear the State into fragments, and "Old Norway" will bend his purpose to our desires. Your Hamlet will become my son; no other son will ever be born to me. His princely future lies in your hands, Gertrude. Together, we will persuade him not to go back to Wittenberg and lead a bookish life. At our side, he will become a seasoned prince, fit to share my power as I grow old,—certain to win the election after my death."

Here his self control broke. "Gertrude," he said

. . . paused . . . spoke her name again . . . was silent and held out his arms.

She went slowly, but straight into them. He sobbed over her head. She actually saw nothing, felt nothing, guessed nothing but tenderness and solace in his eyes or in his gesture. Perhaps he was sincere for the moment, perhaps he had even forgotten his guilt for that instant. He had refrained from unholy expression of love for this woman so long, that perhaps he had, just then, forgotten every evil thing in the universe. She thought his sob was one of reverence.

"Mother of God, I thank thee," she murmured, and, a little later, "Hamlet's father has sent you to save my boy and me."

At that he turned his face quickly from her.

She went back alone to her closet and kissed the stone wall once more,—this time, as one salutes a child when one comes home to stay.

CHAPTER II

SHE had known and moderately liked Claudius so long, that she felt no repulsion at the thought of marrying him. She felt as myriads of women do feel toward men whom they might or might not be willing to marry, according to the trend of circumstances.

The fact that King Hamlet's death had occurred so recently scarcely counted at all with her as a deterrent, nor just then did the love which she had felt for him count in that way. His love, his marriage to her, his life with her, his death, his son,—most of all, the fact that his son was also her's,—they were all separate forces flooding together in one great current of necessity,—necessity that she should marry Claudius.

Soon? . . . "Oh yes," said Claudius to some whispered question of hers, "At once, before any disturbance can arise, or any movement gain strength to oblige me to take to wife a young princess who might bear me half a dozen goodly sons." A woman, in such a predicament as Gertrude found her-self, does not keep a king waiting, especially when she knows there are many princesses standing in line and beckoning to him.

So the fatal mistake was made, and Gertrude, dowager of Denmark, became the wife of Claudius, the King.

Before the ceremony, however, Gertrude did speak to Claudius about the notion, that such a marriage was incestuous. Claudius assured her that he had seen the priests, and everything had been made right as to that. She accepted his statement easily be-cause, in her heart, she held a solemn conviction that angels, "ministers of grace," prompted by the dead King's love, and greater authorities even than the priests, had inspired Claudius to offer the ring which would insure her own and her son's future safety and dignity. Therefore it was with mingled ecstasy and sorrow that this Queen began to tread the pathway to doom.

INTERLUDE

When that phantom Gertrude, who grew to be my intimate there under the pine trees around my home, came to speak of this part of her life, she bade me take note of every item in Shakspeare's rendition of her story. She insisted on my comparing every word which she now said to me with every word which she had been made to say in the drama, or which others had uttered about her. So she and I, in the strangest companionship that ghost and living woman ever shared, communed together over the text.

Gertrude speaks sixty-eight times in Shakspeare's play. Fourteen of her speeches do not directly concern her son. All the others are either spoken to him or about him, or contain some important reference to him. They are all expressions of one poignant passion.

For a little while after the marriage, Gertrude felt that all had been "well and wisely" done. She never doubted Claudius,—no, never once. Perhaps this was not so strange, for she had never seen any man intimately, except as a lover-husband. And Claudius was that, even more, in a way, than King Hamlet had been. Claudius consulted her about everything. He wanted her with him all the time. The trouble was that he wanted her to be with him far more than he wanted to be worthy to have her there. But she did not perceive this flaw in the amber opulence of his joy in her presence.

She did not come so near to loving him, as she had to loving the dead King, but she clung to him from that sense of wifely loyalty, which in her took almost the place of wifely love. Perhaps, the ultimate truth was that no man ever quite developed in her the full blown passion of love. If that were the case, she did not know it. If she had ever had that vague consciousness of vacancy, in the very Universe above and around human existence, which haunts most women who have never wholly loved a man, she had referred this mysterious sensation to the realm of superstitious fear and fancy. She had not thought of it, as betokening an absolute loss of possible experience.

When the proper time had arrived, King Claudius held an audience in the biggest and most splendid room of state in the castle, and there, to the assembled glory of the Danish nobility, he formally presented Gertrude as again and henceforth to be the Queen, "the imperial jointress of this war-like state."

Questioning eyes were bent upon him as he spoke, but the question was not unfriendly in most of them, and, as he went on, there was that, in the general glance, which made him bold to utter his final conviction that as to this marriage—

> "Nor have we herein barr'd
> Your better wisdoms, which have freely gone
> With this affair along."

When he had got through with this part of his address, during which his breath had been rather labored once or twice, he spoke more easily,—concerning public matters, and here Coleridge, centuries later, found a "certain appropriate majesty" in what he said. He gave instructions to ambassadors whom he was sending to Norway. The dead King Hamlet had fought a duel with one Fortinbras, who must have been a brother of the Norwegian king. He had been "thereto pricked on by a most emulate pride," and he had killed his adversary. A "sealed compact" had been prepared by the terms of which each was pledged, in case he were the vanquished one, to forfeit to the other some large territory belonging to himself. This compact was in accord with "law and heraldry" as then administered, and the spoils of the combat were duly made over to the Danish sovereign, after the death of the elder Fortinbras. This duel had occurred on the day that Prince Hamlet was born. It had been a terrible day for Gertrude.

Gertrude of Denmark

Young Fortinbras, son of the dead man, was now bestirring himself in Norway, getting together an army, and Claudius feared that he intended to take forcible possession, if he could, of the lands which had been lost to his inheritance by the fatal issue of his father's duel. So the ambassadors were despatched to suggest to "Old Norway" that it would be well for him to constrain his impetuous nephew to keep the peace with Denmark.

After this business was finished, Laertes, son of Polonius the Lord Chamberlain, asked permission of Claudius to return to France where he had formerly spent much time, for what particular purpose we are not told. Prodigal of words and of incidents is Shakspeare often, but he wastes none to relate or to explain what he seems to consider unimportant for us to know, or perhaps what he thinks the world can guess at shrewdly enough without his help.

Polonius backed up his son's request, and Claudius gave consent to the young man's departure.

Next in due order of procedure, Claudius turned his face towards Hamlet, who stood not far from the throne. Robed entirely in black, he looked among the gay clad noblemen, like a blot from midnight upon a sunset sky. Claudius signed to the Prince to approach and called him "my cousin," and "my son."

Insistently, yet in a tone of tender courtesy such as befitted a queen and a mother, not a petitioner, Gertrude broke into the talk, saying,

"Good Hamlet, cast thy nighted colour off,
And let thine eye look like a friend on Denmark.
Do not forever, with thy vailed lids
Seek for thy noble father in the dust;
Thou know'st 'tis common; all that lives must die,
Passing through nature to eternity."

Her speech is to be understood in the light of the historical fact, recorded by Knight, that it was not customary for Danes, of that period, to mourn publicly for "their nearest and dearest relatives and friends." Therefore, she and Claudius were not making an unusual objection to a usual habit, when they besought Hamlet to make less show of sorrow for his father's death. They were entreating him to avoid such eccentric behavior, as might lead people to think him a man subject to gusts of passion and regardless of settled decorum. Moreover, scarlet was the color worn by Danes of royal station. For Hamlet to appear, at court, in black seemed, to his mother's anxious fancy, like a direct repudiation of the princely rank, to secure which for him she had married, and which Claudius was just proffering to him.

Hamlet answered his mother's reminder, that the death of a father was a common bereavement, by saying in a tone laden with mockery of the idea that that fact could console him, "Ay madam, it is common."

Gertrude asked, "If it be, why seems it so particular with thee?"

Only unsuspecting innocence could have prompted this question. No accomplice in either murder or adultery would thus have sought to probe the heart of her victim's son.

When Hamlet had finished his next speech, Claudius took up the theme at length, and Gertrude smiled contentedly as she listened, for among other things he said,

> "Let the world take note,
> You are the most immediate to our throne,
> And with no less nobility of love
> Than that which dearest father bears his son
> Do I impart to you."

He went on to beseech Hamlet not to return to Wittenberg, but to remain

Gertrude of Denmark

"Here in the cheer and comfort of our eye,
Our chiefest courtier, cousin, and our son."

The phantom Gertrude still believed that Claudius
was practically sincere in this speech.

I think that she was right about that. Claudius
had not then begun to be afraid lest Hamlet should
learn and avenge his father's murder; and he was
probably hugging to his soul the fancy that, by good-
ness to the son, he might not only please the mother
but could make some atonement to Heaven for his
sin. It seems probable, moreover, that there was
some other impulse moving Claudius in this hour.
It was one that, in the nature of things, could hardly
have long remained in active existence within him.
But I, the present chronicler, think that just then
this impulse was very strong. Claudius could love
as well as desire.

Though selfish desire had at last overcome him,
still, on the whole, there had been much moral worth
in the denied love which he had felt, during thirty
years, for Gertrude. And at the worst, there was
much constancy in it. The man, who could feel such
an affection as that, could feel others.

The elements of good and ill were so mixed in him
that although there had been times when he had hated

the boy with a jealous and, occasionally, with a temperamental hatred, there had been other times when he loved Gertrude's child. Then also Hamlet had that charm which always has and always will work emotional wonders; whether its possessor be morally good or bad. In a child such a charm is irresistible. Claudius had felt it.

Facing his brother's son, now grown to manhood, the heart of Claudius, I doubt not, yearned towards him with a great yearning. He possessed the mother,—Oh, if only he could put aside every hindering memory and possess the son also as his own!

Such, I believe, was the main drift of his feeling on that audience day.

There is another element in human nature which may have influenced him. That which a man has injured, he ordinarily either hates or loves. Just then the childless Claudius probably both loved and longed to love the young man who was nearest to him in blood, and whom he had most injured.

Wanting to feel that she would count for something, in the moment when her son should weigh one thing against another and decide whether he would be a scholar in foreign lands, or a prince in Denmark, Gertrude gently seconded the King's plea saying—

"Let not thy mother lose her prayers, Hamlet,"
"I pray thee stay with us."

He consented to her prayer, and Gertrude, now a
satisfied mother, became, absurdly contradictory as
it may seem, at once the sad widow of a dead man
and the thankful wife of a living one.

When the audience had ended and Hamlet was
left alone, his soul plunged into a solitude more vacant of life than the empty chamber in which he
stood.

He gave utterance to the age-long cry of youth in
such moments—the cry for death;

> "O that this too, too solid flesh would melt,
> Thaw, and resolve itself into a dew!
> Or that the Everlasting had not fix'd
> His canon 'gainst self-slaughter!
>   O God!   O God!"

Still talking to himself, he then spoke of the time
which had elapsed since his father's death, first declaring that two months had slipped away, then saying it was not yet two months, and concluding with
the statement that his mother had married "within
the month" of the death's occurrence. One may

fairly conclude, from all this, that it was now some six or seven weeks since King Hamlet had died and two or three after Gertrude's marriage.

In this soliloquy the Prince expressed abhorrence of the marriage as incestuous and therefore abominable in itself. But he hated it also because it seemed to contradict the appearance of his mother's former life, as he had observed and understood it. He had seen her whole existence dominated, as he thought, by eager as well as tender affection for his father. Probably he did not know that in a woman, constituted like his mother, tenderness and amiability united might sincerely, and even unconsciously, take on the pleasing semblance of passionate delight. Now, bewildered by his reminiscences, Hamlet was unable to imagine any decent feeling which could have induced his widowed mother to marry at all.

It is a little difficult to see why Hamlet did not think of himself as an inciting cause for the Queen's action. It was not because he was indifferent to the princely rank or to the position of sovereignty. Probably it was because he had not thought out the situation and had not realized the consequences, which would have resulted to himself, had Claudius married some other woman. Moreover, he had always taken his mother's love for himself so much as a thing of course that he had failed to perceive its depth; and life had not developed in him a sensitive sympathy for the condition of womanhood, as such. He did not appreciate the special burdens imposed upon womanhood by nature, and he had no conception of its pathetic adaptability and its co-existent inadaptability to the various social customs which bounded or directed its movement. Neither his knowledge nor his philosophy furnished him with any clue to his mother's character.

His thought of marriage was rather crude. He saw it largely in its physical aspect. His uncle was not handsome,—his father had been. Claudius was a satyr to a Hyperion compared to the dead King. How could she turn from the memory of the one to the presence of the other? So he brooded over what had happened.

At no moment, however, in this hour of reflection, did he utter a word of suspicion that his mother's marriage had been the detestable consummation of an adulterous union.

While Hamlet was still chewing the cud of his fancies, three young men came in upon him. He spoke to one of them in a manner that denoted former friendly acquaintance, although it showed that they two had not met for some time, as it expressed a mo-

mentary doubt whether the man thus greeted really
were the Horatio whom he took him to be. He gave
a pleasant but more distant salutation to the others,
who were Marcellus and Bernardo, officers of the
Castle Guard. That courtesy ended, he began to
talk eagerly to Horatio, who told him that he had
come to Elsinore to see the late King's funeral.
Horatio thus revealed the fact that he had been in
the neighborhood for several weeks without attempt-
ing to see the Prince.

Undeterred by this, or any other reason which
might have prompted reserve, Hamlet readily seized
the opportunity to complain of his own mother. Of
Horatio's avowed motive for visiting Elsinore, he
said,

"I pray thee, do not mock me, fellow-student;
I think it was to see my mother's wedding,"

And to Horatio's helpless admission concerning
that wedding, "Indeed, my lord, it followed hard
upon," Hamlet made a reply which was witty rather
than becoming in a son,

"Thrift, thrift, Horatio! the funeral bak'd meats
Did coldly furnish forth the marriage tables."

With more savage emphasis he went on,

"Would I had met my dearest foe in Heaven
Or ever I had seen that day, Horatio!"

Hamlet had but a few seconds more of breathing
time allowed him, ere he received a new and tremen-
dous shock.

His companions told him that, on the preceding
night, they had, all three together, seen what they
believed to be the Ghost of his father walking silently
before them on the battlements of the castle, and
that Marcellus and Bernardo had seen it twice on
previous occasions.

After much careful inquiry about the apparition
and all the attendant circumstances, Hamlet swore
the men to secrecy and agreed to meet them in the
coming midnight, promising to watch with them on
the ramparts, and declaring that if the Ghost should
appear, wearing his father's shape, he would "speak
to it though Hell itself should gape and bid him hold
his peace."

CHAPTER III

IN the afternoon of this audience day, Laertes finished his preparations for his departure to France, and being for a time alone with his sister, he spoke to her of Hamlet and told her that the Prince's attentions had not been of such a nature as to prove that he meant to marry her. Also the brother made it plain that, even if Hamlet did desire marriage, it was extremely unlikely that he could bring it about.

INTERLUDE

"No one," said the phantom Gertrude, when we were studying this scene, as Shakspeare gives it, "can understand Ophelia aright, who does not fully realize how cogent were the reasons given her by her father and brother for withdrawing herself from the intimacy which she had accorded to Hamlet. Nobody can understand me aright who does not also realize that of all this pressure upon the girl, I was then ignorant. And no one can understand my son aright, who does not see that, vehement as was his

wooing, he did dally with the purposes of love, and
did postpone the action which, by committing him
to marriage, might have brought him into contradiction with 'the main voice of Denmark.' Her
father and brother did but do their duty to a motherless maiden, when they bade her refuse the courtship
of a prince who had not asked her to be his wife."

The phantom sighed,—then smiled a little indul-
gently, "I think," she said, "that if Hamlet could
have married Ophelia in some single minute, and
have performed the whole ceremony himself, he
would have done it,—unless indeed, the figure of her
father had shown itself peeping around the corner,
before the knot was fast tied."

It should be noted here, and the fact carefully
weighed, that at this time, Hamlet had not learned
the manner of his father's death. It cannot therefore be supposed that it was because of any scruple
about drawing Ophelia into the meshes of his own
tragic destiny, that he had delayed proposing marriage until her father and brother had become seriously alarmed.

No fine natured, well nurtured girl could fail to
be moved by the tenderly spoken counsel which
Laertes gave to his sister—

Gertrude of Denmark

"For Hamlet and the trifling of his favour,
Hold it a fashion and a toy in blood,
A violet in the youth of primy nature,
Forward, not permanent, sweet, not lasting,
The perfume and suppliance of a minute;
No more."

Ophelia sighed her heart out in four little words
of question,
"No more but so?"
Then her brother gently unfolded the whole situation to her and revealed its meaning.   He did it with
evident purpose to be just to Hamlet, and also not to
shock her with too bald a statement of the peril in
which she stood, nor to drive her into antagonism by
unwarranted suspicion of the man whom she loved.
He said,

"Perhaps he loves you now,
And now no soil, nor cautel doth besmirch
The virtue of his will; but you must fear,
His greatness weighed, his will is not his own;
For he himself is subject to his birth,
He may not, as unvalued persons do,
Carve for himself, for on his choice depends
The safety and health of this whole state;
And therefore must his choice be circumscribed

[39]

Unto the voice and yielding of that body,
Whereof he is the head.   Then if he says he loves
    you,
It fits your wisdom so far to believe it,
As he in his particular act and place
May give his saying deed; which is no further
Than the main voice of Denmark goes withal."

Ophelia was silent for a while after Laertes said
this.   She rose from her seat, moved across the
room, took up a bit of unfinished embroidery, laid
it down again on the table, and stood still with her
face turned from her brother.   He knew by her silence, that all was as he had supposed.   Hamlet had
not only omitted to tell either of her kinsmen that his
purpose was that of marriage, he had never even
spoken a decisive word to her.

At last the girl came resolutely toward Laertes,
and he saw that her eyes were full of tears.   He
steadied his soul, and spoke again at some length
warning her of the danger of permitting a close intimacy with a lover, who was not an avowed suitor
for her hand.   His words were still gentle and sufficiently reserved, but all the time she stood motionless, looking straight at him.   He felt that he had
never been in the presence of such courage as hers.

He was stabbing her, and she stood there with un-shielded breast receiving her death-blow.

When he had quite finished, Ophelia spoke of the moral issue involved. She uttered a touching protest against what has since been called the double standard, saying

"I shall the effect of this good lesson keep,
As watchman to my heart. But, good my brother,
Do not, as some ungracious pastors do,
Show me the steep and thorny way to heaven,
While, like a puff'd and reckless libertine,
Himself the primrose path of dalliance treads,
And recks not his own rede."

Thus worthily did the sister counter the brother, in the discussion of those high themes which pertain to vital conduct. Here was a woman capable of clear sight and true thought. Whatever may have been Hamlet's purposes at this juncture in his career, the impulse of his affection had gone straight to a golden mark. Calamity came later when he began to doubt the validity of his own soul's endorsement of his love.

Polonius came in rather abruptly, and his entrance took from Laertes the necessity of making very much reply to his sister. He gave a proper greeting to his father. Ophelia retired a little space from both men, sat down beside the table and, fumbling the embroidery again with trembling fingers, managed to hide her startled wet eyes from her father's sight.

Polonius made a solemn yet sensible address to his son for five long minutes, while that young fellow stood stock still, seeming to listen but really thinking, in a whirling, bewildered fashion, of all that had passed between him and his sister.

He made his manners at last to his father, and got himself over to Ophelia, who rose to meet him, and put her arms around his neck. He spoke low, but Polonius, who had come up close, heard him say

"Farewell, Ophelia; and remember well
What I have said to you."

So soon as the lad was actually gone, Polonius cried a little, and then, controlling the sob in his throat, and patting his daughter on her shoulder, asked,

"What is't, Ophelia, he hath said to you?"

Frankly, though timidly, she answered, "So please you, something touching the Lord Hamlet."

Gertrude of Denmark

"Marry, well bethought," cried the old man, and added from his own store of knowledge on the subject,

" 'Tis told me, he hath very oft of late
    Given private time to you, and you yourself
    Have of your audience been most free and boun-
        teous;
    If it be so—as so 'tis put on me,
    And that in way of caution—I must tell you
    You do not understand yourself so clearly
    As it behooves my daughter and your honour.
    What is between you? Give me up the truth."

The father was clearly within his right,—his speech was wholly in the line of his duty. Ophelia had not, until this hour of agony, realized the awful-ness of Hamlet's silences; her consciousness had not been awake as to what he had not said,—drowned in her rapture at listening to what he did say. She struggled to yield up to her father only the sacred truth of his speech,

"He hath, my lord," she answered honestly, "of late made many tenders of his affection to me."

This brought from the anxious father the blunt but necessary inquiry,

"Do you believe his tenders, as you call them?"

"I do not know, my lord, what I should think."

Polonius could have cried afresh over this innocent and helpless confession. He suddenly hugged and kissed his child. "Marry, I'll teach you; think yourself a baby," he half sobbed, half chuckled, and then spoke on, rather roughly, in order to keep from becoming too soft for her good.

She tried again to persuade him and herself that things were not really, as she now knew that they did seem to be.

"My lord," she began in her sweet reiterating way, "he hath importun'd me with love in honourable fashion."

His old fingers tapped her lips with the touch of yearning affection, but he brought his eyebrows together in a frown.

"Ay, fashion you may call it, go to, go to."

Notwithstanding his frown, his voice was a caressing sound.

She made her last effort to establish a truth which was not the whole truth. She made it plaintively, desperately, but sincerely. Without repeating either the name or uttering the pronoun which would indicate her lover, she said,

"And hath given countenance to his speech, my lord,
With almost all the holy vows of heaven."

Polonius choked over the lovely pitifulness of his
girl, but the full truth had become only too evident.
Hamlet had not said, "Let me tell your father that
you love me." Polonius had now no honorable
choice but to forbid his child to allow Hamlet any
further easy access to her society. He did not, for
a single instant, dally with the temptation to make
gain for himself by permitting her to become the
mistress of the foremost prince of the realm.

Ophelia submitted to the authority which was
compact of righteousness.

"I shall obey, my lord," she said.

A shadow henceforth darkened over Ophelia's
young, idealizing imagination. She was unable to
put entirely away, from her fond conception of Hamlet, the consciousness which her father and brother
had awakened in her,—the consciousness that it had
been ignoble in him to make love to her without proffering the wedding ring. But she did not want to
think of any phase of his character or conduct which
seemed ignoble.

Gertrude of Denmark

She loved him so much that she desired merely to suffer because she was separated from him, and not to blame him at all either for the separation or the suffering. She desired this with that quiet, motionless ardor, which infuses thwarted love with what is perhaps its most deadly energy. To know that a lover has a great fault, and to try not to see it,—that is to walk with closed eyes along a rocky path.

Ophelia hushed her sorrowful longings by prayer, and by permitting herself to feel every increasing thrill of love that was simply tender and unquestioning.

But the weight pressing in her heart grew daily and hourly heavier.

Worst of all were the moments when she had to refuse Hamlet's visits and return his letters;—for he did ask twice to see her, and twice he wrote to her, in the two months following the day that her father talked with her about him.

She never considered the possibility of disobeying her father or of disregarding her brother's counsel. It cannot be said that she was even tempted to do so. She had no prompting impulse that way.

It was not merely her father who had forbidden her to entertain an unlawful love. Her own soul forbade her, because her soul was fashioned in accord with Universal law and order; and, in her thought, Universal law and order had to do with a woman's chaste preparation to be a wife and mother, the paternity of whose child could never be in doubt.

Ophelia's father possessed some classical knowledge. Her mother, who had had the "chaste unsmirched brows" which still beautifully dominated the memory of Laertes, had now been dead a year; but Ophelia had heard her father speak to her of Caesar and Caesar's wife, and she knew that a woman should be above suspicion.

Blameless love at a distance from Hamlet, and close approach by prayer to Heaven,—these were the exercises with which she sought to strengthen herself to endure.

CHAPTER IV

AT the appointed midnight hour, after Laertes left for France, Hamlet went to the ramparts and met Horatio and the two officers of the Guard. They took up their watch on a platform flanking a turret, in which there were, above their heads, only two or three narrow slits for windows. No light gleamed from these openings.

They heard trumpets blare and guns fired in a more distant part of the castle. The noise indicated that the Danish King, at that moment, was drinking "Rhenish wine." Hamlet detested the custom of such a midnight carousal and the proclamation thereof in that manner.

The watchers stood leaning against the turret walls. The sky was clouded. The darkness seemed thick in front and over them as, staring into space, they waited and wondered.

At last, an image appeared, at the corner of a passage way between the tower behind them and one a little farther removed in the direction opposite to that, in which the firing of guns had occurred.

Gertrude of Denmark

The image looked to be lighted by a glow emanating from itself. They saw it plainly and it resembled the dead King.

Hamlet hailed it; "King, father, royal Dane." He implored it to speak to him. He made loving entreaty.

The image was silent, but it beckoned, as though summoning him to follow it—where?

His companions begged him not to go with this shape into the darkness.

"Why, what should be the fear?" he exclaimed.

"I do not set my life at a pin's fee;
And for my soul, what can it do to that,
Being a thing immortal as itself?
It waves me forth again; I'll follow it."

Horatio expostulated, offering direful suggestions;

"What if it tempt you toward the flood, my lord,
Or to the dreadful summit of the cliff,
That beetles o'er his base into the sea,
And there assume some other horrible form,
Which might deprive your sovereignty of reason
And draw you into madness?"

Hamlet called directly to the shape, "Go on, I'll follow thee."

The men tried to restrain him forcibly. "You shall not go," said Horatio.

Hamlet retorted,

> "My fate cries out,
> And makes each petty artery in this body
> As hardy as the Nemean lion's nerve.
> Still am I called.—Unhand me, gentlemen,
> By heaven, I'll make a ghost of him that lets me."

He went with that supernaturally lighted figure into the invisible spaces among the turrets.

Although he was thus companioned, and indeed, because he was thus companioned, his was the most lonesome march that mortal ever made.

He heard his own feet touch the stony pathway which he trod. But he heard no sound from that thing of dreadful beauty moving before him.

On a platform, which was as much detached as was architecturally possible, from any building, Hamlet stopped, and cried, "I'll go no further."

Then a voice issued from the spectral lips of the shape, so addressed, and said, "Mark me. My hour is almost come, when I to sulphurous and tormenting flames, must render up myself."

This was the first message from the world beyond the grave, which came to Hamlet's ears.

Gertrude of Denmark

What did it do to Hamlet's soul, which he had
thought, a moment earlier, to be immune from spiritual injury?

"Alas, poor ghost!" he moaned.

The next message delivered to him by the spectral
Shadow, bade him to "pity not," but to "revenge."

Then that Appearance which resembled an image
fashioned out of earthly mould, told the son that he
was his father's spirit, and that ghost though he were,
he was the inhabitant of a region, whence he had
been permitted to escape for only a few hours, and
in which he suffered frightful torture, as of the flesh,
in punishment for "foul crimes" which he had committed in the flesh.

He also told the son just how Claudius had murdered him by pouring poison into the porches of his
ears, as he lay asleep in the garden. And thus, he
said, he was "of life, of crown, of queen at once
despatch'd." This phrase, taken by itself, would
indicate that Claudius had not got possession, in any
way, of the Queen before he had killed her husband.

Other statements do, however, suggest that the
ghostly speaker had come to suspect, and perhaps
to believe, that his "most seeming-virtuous queen"
had been shamefully won to a wicked love, while his
now incorporeal soul had been united to material

substance. But there is no word in this scene or elsewhere, in the whole of Shakspeare's dramatic rendition of the story, which even intimates that the King, during his existence upon the earth, had ever doubted his wife's fidelity.

And the Ghost, although he raged and raved in this midnight hour against Gertrude's marriage, did not quite definitely accuse her of having committed the adulterate act. His plainest speech ran thus,

"That incestuous, that adulterate beast, [meaning
        Claudius]
    With witchcraft of his wit, with traitorous gifts,—
    O wicked wit and gifts, that have the power
    So to seduce!—won to his shameful lust
    The will of my most seeming-virtuous queen."

The Ghost brought forward no memory of the past, he related no incident newly recalled which, though it had aroused no suspicion in him when it occurred, had now come to wear the aspect of guilt to his spectral vision.

In view of this fact, and of no directly phrased accusation, is it not lawful to conclude that the word "will" does not necessarily convey a charge of wrong action?

Gertrude of Denmark

INTERLUDE

"Oh," cried the phantom Gertrude indignantly. "Whatever Claudius may have done, there was one indecorous thing he never would have done. He would never have made his mistress the queen of Denmark."

The Ghost indulged in some self-eulogy to the effect that he was very superior to his brother, whom he called "a wretch whose natural gifts were poor" compared to his own. He also expressed great horror of Gertrude's second marriage. He said to the Prince,

"Let not the royal bed of Denmark be
A couch for luxury and damned incest.
But, howsoever thou pursuest this act,
Taint not thy mind, nor let thy soul contrive
Against thy mother aught; leave her to heaven,
And to those thorns that in her bosom lodge,
To prick and sting her."

Saying that he must not, he did tell much of the torment to which he was subjected, in that purgatorial limbo where he had been sentenced, "for a certain term to walk the night, and for the day confin'd to fast in fires,"

Gertrude of Denmark

                                   "But that I am forbid
To tell the secrets of my prison house,
I could a tale unfold whose lightest word
Would harrow up thy soul, freeze thy young blood,
Make thy two eyes, like stars, start from their
      spheres,
Thy knotted and combined locks to part,
And each particular hair to stand an end,
Like quills upon the fretful porcupine;
But this eternal blazon must not be
To ears of flesh and blood."

He spoke of the approaching hour when back to torture he must go; and he dwelt bitterly on the consequence to himself that, "by a brother's hand," he had been sent unshriven to face the Court of Judgment beyond the mortal bar,—saying,

    "Thus was I, . . .
      Cut off even in the blossoms of my sin,
      Unhousel'd, disappointed, unanel'd,
      No reckoning made, but sent to my account
      With all my imperfections on my head:
      O, horrible!   O, horrible!   Most horrible!
      If thou hast nature in thee, bear it not."

With every possible emphasis and, amid emotional ejaculations falling from Hamlet's lips, the Ghost called thus upon his son:

"List, list, O list.
If thou didst ever thy dear father love—
Revenge his foul and most unnatural murther.
Murther most foul, as in the best it is;
But this most foul, strange and unnatural."

At this stupendous revelation of terror in heaven, of wickedness on earth, and of a hell that matched each of them in all elements of dreadful portent, the young man's flesh trembled, his heart fainted, his soul staggered, and his mind grew incapable of apprehending what was true or what was false; and henceforth, only now and then did he see clearly either what was good or what was beautiful.

He cried out in his agony when the Ghost had left him,

"O all you host of heaven!   O earth!   What else?
And shall I couple hell?   O, fie!   Hold, hold, my
    heart;
And you, my sinews, grow not instant old;
But bear me stiffly up.   Remember thee!
Ay, thou poor ghost, while memory holds a seat
In this distracted globe."

Then the impulse came upon him "to wipe from the table of" his memory,

"All saws of books, all forms, all pressures past;
 That youth and observation copied there;"

so that the Ghost's commandment, and that a commandment to revenge, alone should "live within the book and volume of" his brain.

I, the recorder of the phantom Gertrude's story, do not know just what she thought concerning the Gospel commandment to love and forgive one's enemies, even though it should become one's duty to execute justice upon them; but I do know that the main body, of Shakspeare's exposition of life, is a triumphant presentation of the infinite value of that Gospel doctrine of forgiveness.

"O most pernicious woman," cried Hamlet at once, as all human images became confounded in universal blackness.

Everything, except his vivid consciousness of the Ghost, being thus blent in a panorama of evil moving around him, Hamlet speedily developed the impulse to become himself something strange, odd, and deformed from nature.

But, instantly after this impulse had begun to direct his faculties and to reveal itself in speech to

Horatio and the officers of the Guard, who had now come where the Ghost had left him upon the parapet, an instinct of caution arose within him. He swore his companions not to tell anyone that he had walked and talked that night with a spectral figure, even if they should see him carrying out the purpose, which he had already disclosed to them, of putting on "an antic disposition."

When Hamlet began to administer the oath of secrecy, he was interrupted by the voice of the Ghost coming up from beneath the stones on which they stood, and saying distinctly the one word "Swear."

Hamlet staggered and faltered for a moment, and then he called downward in a tone of bravado,

"Ah, ha, boy! Say'st thou so? Art thou there, true-penny?"

He began to repeat the oath again, "Swear by my sword," he said.

From below his feet came up the awful reiterating command, "Swear."

Hamlet drew the men to another spot on the castle rampart. He repeated the formula, and twice again sounded that terrible echo from the underworld, "Swear."

"Rest, rest, perturbed spirit," cried Hamlet at last.

After this, he recovered somewhat of his usual

bearing and spoke to the men with winning courtesy—

"So, gentlemen,
With all my love I do commend me to you;
And what so poor a man as Hamlet is
May do, to express his love and friending to you,
God willing, shall not lack.   Let us go in together."

These words spoken, the horror seized him again. He repeated his entreaty that they should never reveal the fact that a terrible thing had come to pass that night.   And, last of all, his wavering soul forced from his lips an unheroic, unpatriotic sigh,—

"The time is out of joint;—O cursed spite,
That ever I was born to set it right!"

Here was no girding of the loins to do a great cleansing deed for Denmark, either in the way of sublime forgiveness, of sternly executed justice,—or even of angry revenge.

He was now stumbling on his mental pathway,— but he could not bear to be physically alone, "Nay, come," he said, "let's go together."

CHAPTER V

DURING the eight or nine following weeks, Hamlet did put on an "antic disposition" and people began to think him insane. Many reports of his wild action and his wilder speech were brought to Ophelia. They saddened and frightened her. She cried over them in secret and prayed so much that it might truly be said that, in the background of her mind, a prayer for him was always saying itself.

Except when obliged to be in the castle she stayed closely at home, but she often caught sight of him as he came out and went through the courtyards and corridors of the palace. When she saw him, her lips without her will whispered to her heart, "How beautiful he is!" If she were alone and secure from being seen, then she always fell on her knees and breathed a special prayer for his soul.

She loved him for the beauty of his face, as one loves a blossom; she loved him for the sweetness of his voice, as one loves the sound of music; but more than for either of these things, she still loved him for what she had once imagined to be the essence of his spirit.

Gertrude of Denmark

It is probable that it was customary in Denmark, at this period, to neglect insane people, to such an extent, that they were often forced to go about very scantily or filthily clad. It is possible that, as a consequence of this habit as to appearance, the less seriously afflicted lunatics, and also those persons, who suffered merely from an imitative hysteria, would themselves rend and soil their garments. It is certain that, in due time, it became the conventional mode of representing insanity, on the stage, to show it in grossly disordered dress.

So, were it because of real insanity, or because of the desire to imitate what he had seen, either in life or in the theatre, Hamlet did something one morning, and Ophelia fled to her father for mental guidance and personal protection. She found him, just rising from a desk in his main office. He saw at once that his daughter had come to him because she was in trouble.

"How now, Ophelia! What's the matter?" he asked, holding out his hand.

She told her story; saying that as she sat sewing in her closet,

"Lord Hamlet, with his doublet all unbrac'd;
No hat upon his head; his stockings foul'd,

Gertrude of Denmark

Ungartered and down-gyved to his ankle;
Pale as his shirt, his knees knocking each other;
And with a look so piteous in purport
As if he had been loosed out of hell
To speak of horrors,—he comes before me."

Polonius drew the inevitable deduction. "Mad
for thy love?" he said in a questioning tone; and
Ophelia made the natural reply, "My lord, I do not
know; but truly, I do fear it."

Then, stammering a little, but resolutely, she gave
a detailed description of all that Hamlet had done,
holding her by the wrist "hard," while he silently
gazed upon her for a long time, speaking no word,
and then she said,

"He raised a sigh so piteous and profound
As it did seem to shatter all his bulk
And end his being: that done, he lets me go,
And, with his head over his shoulder turn'd,
He seem'd to find his way without his eyes;
For out o' doors he went without their help,
And, to the last, bended their light on me."

The feelings of the father, as he listened, were di-
vided between solicitude for his daughter and loyal
interest in behalf of the afflicted Prince.

"Have you given him any hard words of late?" he asked.

Ophelia answered, "No, my good lord, but, as you did command, I did repel his letters, and denied his access to me."

"That hath made him mad," said Polonius gravely. Yet, knowing that he had done only what a father should do, even though it were his prince who had suffered in consequence, he reminded both himself and her of the righteousness of his motives, saying, "I feared he did but trifle and meant to wrack thee."

Nevertheless, in generous fashion he continued to blame himself as one who might have been over suspicious.

Ophelia spoke no word to all this, and with equal silence she listened when he said that he should go frankly to the King and Queen and tell the whole story.

Undoubtedly his busy brain, always ready at making conjectures and schemes, did not let his heart feel sorry for Hamlet long, before it whispered of the chance that the royal consent might now be gained to the marriage of Hamlet and Ophelia.

Shortly before this day, Gertrude had suggested to Claudius that they should ask Rosencrantz and

Guildenstern, two of her son's school friends, to come
to the court and see if they could divert the unhappy
Prince's mind. Still, although she desired their coming, she dreaded it vaguely—not because she dis-
trusted the two handsome young fellows, whom she
had liked in their boyhood, but, because since all
which concerned her son was then going wrong, she
had become acutely apprehensive that everything
would continue to go wrong.

When the men arrived, however, and were ushered
into her presence and that of the King, she felt a momentary joy in their slim figures, straight features
and graceful demeanor, a joy which aroused a sensation of hopefulness. Gay, courteous youth bowed
before her, and it seemed impossible that it should
not bring the cup of renewal to her lips.

She greeted these visitors with a graciousness, in
which maternal dignity was divinely blent with a
younger sort of womanly charm. As they knelt to
kiss her hands, she said of the Prince,

"Good gentlemen, he hath much talk'd of you,
    And sure I am two men there are not living
    To whom he more adheres."

She and the King both requested these lads to take
up their abode at the court, and assured them of

gratitude and recompensing favor, if they should succeed in gaining Hamlet's confidence. After receiving satisfactory replies from them, Gertrude said,

"Thanks, Guildenstern and gentle Rosencrantz:
And I beseech you instantly to visit
My too much changed son";

then turning towards the attendants waiting at a convenient distance in the room, she continued

"Go, some of you,
And bring these gentlemen where Hamlet is."

Guildenstern made answer, "Heaven make our presence and our practices pleasant and helpful to him!"

She caught her breath, and her whispered "Ay, Amen," was almost inaudible.

After the young men with their escort had left the chamber, Polonius entered. He announced the return from Norway of the Danish ambassadors, and also managed to speak apart to the King, saying, "I have found the very cause of Hamlet's lunacy."

Claudius did not shrink from the disclosure which Polonius might make. Whether, out of belief that his own guilt had been hidden beyond the Chamberlain's power of discovery, or in consequence of measureless ability to do the necessary thing, he courted such disclosure.

"O speak of that"; he said, "that do I long to hear."

But Polonius deliberately suggested the postponement of his revelation till after a hearing should be given to the ambassadors, and left the room to summon those envoys into the royal presence. So soon as he was gone, Claudius rising from his seat stepped to Gertrude's side and, putting his hand on her shoulder, said,

"He tells me, my sweet queen, that he hath found
The head and source of all your son's distemper."

A change of feeling shook her soul and her brief joy faded. She drew herself a little away, and looking at him steadily, though with frightened eyes, she uttered her hitherto unacknowledged thought,

"I doubt it is no other but the main,—
His father's death, and our o'er hasty marriage."

The eyes of Claudius grew hard and cold. He said simply, "Well, we shall sift him," and turned from her. In a moment more, he whirled back, lifted her to her feet, took her in his arms and held her close for a few seconds.

The attendants, remaining in the more distant spaces of the great hall, meanwhile, heard nothing and, as it is likely that, bored in the performance of their statue-like duty, they cared nothing about it all, they probably actually saw not much more than they properly appeared to see of this little scene.

Long before the ambassadors entered, their majesties had withdrawn from each other to their appointed stations of dignity.

The ambassadors made their report. "Old Norway" had learned that his nephew Fortinbras was intending to attack Denmark, had rebuked him, and the young man had submitted and decided to bestow his war-like attentions upon "the Polack."

Claudius expressed his gratification; that business ended, and the ambassadors gone, the moment for Polonius arrived. He came forward eagerly to develop his theory, but he was prolix in the development.

Gertrude felt that something would break within, or else would explode outside her, if he did not hurry his speech and she interrupted him. She rushed at knowledge as she might have cast herself upon the point of a sword. She commanded from the Chamberlain, "More matter with less art."

Polonius stammered in self-vindication, "Madam,

Gertrude of Denmark

I swear I use no art at all," and then meandered on his verbal course as before.

Gertrude grew sick. She had now become aware that the marriage which she had made largely to secure Hamlet's rank, had displeased him deeply and had hurt him in his affections on account of his father. She had even come to sympathize secretly with that hurt. The thing that she dreaded now, was the misery of hearing this old man say in plain words, "Madam, your son is sorry you did not go into the convent."

Of course, she knew that the courtier would veil his meaning so far as the necessities of speech would allow. She knew he never could tell Claudius and herself to their faces that their marriage had driven Hamlet mad. Yet it was this preposterous impossibility which Gertrude feared, while the Chamberlain's words dripped and dropped from his lips.

When he began to speak of his daughter, Gertrude's spirit rose dizzy with relief. Ophelia . . . dear little Ophelia . . . was it all about her, and naught about herself! Still she was in doubt. Denied love for a girl seemed to her to be too simple a cause for such effect as madness in her son.

She did not fully understand Hamlet's character, but she did know that it was a complicated one.

Half unconsciously, she knew that she herself would never have gone mad for love of any man. Half unconsciously also, she attributed to the possession of her son a certain coldness, induced, as she thought, by his philosophizing tendency, which made it unlikely that he would lose the balance of his mind in the whirl of a passion of the primitive sort.

She could more easily believe the thing she dreaded, because she did perceive that his thoughts and feelings about "his father's death and her o'er hasty marriage" were not the outgrowth of primitive passions. They had to do with his philosophic questionings and conceptions. They had to do with the whole of life and with all that he comprehended of the Universe.

Love and marriage themselves were to him crudely simple affairs of emotion, of churchly government and personal necessity;—but second marriage and the second marriage of his mother, his father's widow, a woman of proper age and station for convent life,—that was different; that gave him puzzled thought, which developed disgust.

She knew also that, although Hamlet had really loved his father, it was the death of his father, rather than his own filial affection, which had opened the gates of speculation in his mind and had set the eyes of his spirit peering into the darkest abysses of fathomless mystery.

She did not know that, for months now, he had felt as though the Ghost of his father were still walking beside him as it had done that midnight on the parapets; but, she had intuitively perceived that he was conducting himself like one who was constantly accompanied by a haunting thought which had come to seem, even to her, like an unseen yet real Presence.

Could it be just Ophelia—nothing but Ophelia?

To substantiate his theory, Polonius read to their Majesties from a letter, which Ophelia had submissively rendered up to him, "To the celestial, and my soul's idol, the most beautified Ophelia, In her excellent white bosom these,—"

Gertrude interrupted, "Came this from Hamlet to her?"

"Good madam," protested the old man, "I will be faithful." And after this, Gertrude listened silently to the reading of the rest of the letter, to the brief discussion of the situation by Polonius and King Claudius, and to the long narrative and explanation made by the Lord Chamberlain of what had happened in relation to Hamlet's intimacy with Ophelia, what he had done about it, and part of the reason that he had for his action. She was willing to be convinced, and when at last Claudius turned to ask her, "Do you think 'tis thus?" Gertrude was ready to answer thoughtfully, "It may be, very likely."

Polonius then began to outline his plan that Hamlet and Ophelia should be brought into each other's presence, in such circumstances, that they should think themselves alone and unobserved. He said, "You know, sometimes he walks four hours together, here in the lobby."

"So he does indeed," she whispered.

Ah yes, she knew,—his mother knew what he did. Many were the days when she had contrived to cross the corridor or to linger by a window, either for the purpose of meeting him directly or, unobserved herself, of watching him, as he moved about the castle, and of noting whence he came and whither he went and how he occupied himself.

Claudius decided to carry out the Lord Chamberlain's scheme and subject Hamlet's mentality to the test of a sudden meeting with Ophelia, and just as he said, "We will try it," Gertrude saw her son approaching. "But, look," she murmured, "where sadly the poor wretch comes reading."

She started to go towards him, but Claudius slipped his hand under her arm, and led her away in an opposite direction. The attendants followed in order, two by two, and Polonius remained in the middle space of the room.

He greeted the Prince courteously when he had come near. Hamlet talked wildly to him for a few minutes, and then demanding, apropos of nothing, "Have you a daughter?" he began some uncalled for and unpleasantly impertinent speech about the care of a daughter.

Polonius was either too accustomed to princely incivility to mind it, or too tenderly sorry for the young madman, or too paternally anxious to get him as a husband for his girl, to show offence, even when in reply to his deferential leavetaking, Hamlet made an answer which was equivalent to saying "Good riddance to you."

Rosencrantz and Guildenstern entered just before Polonius went out, and there ensued a long verbal contest between them and the Prince, whom they had been commissioned to amuse and to observe. They did the best they could, trying to serve his nearest relatives, whom they naturally believed to be bent on securing his welfare. But he grew suspicious and irritated as he became inevitably aware that they were putting him through a sort of mental examination and endeavoring to diagnose his case.

Gertrude of Denmark

They finally honestly admitted that they had been sent for by the King and Queen, and because of some knowledge of his, which they did not possess, that admission did not help them to establish relations with him of trustful friendship.

He however became eagerly interested in their account of recent theatrical matters, and his suspicions ceased to occupy his thoughts for a few minutes, during which his manner grew more cordial and frank.

The entrance of Polonius brought mockery back to Hamlet's spirit and he resumed his attitude of supercilious disdain. He again made speeches which could not fail to convince the father that the daughter was foremost in the dance of his reckless fancies.

Polonius, as well as Rosencrantz and Guildenstern, announced to the Prince the coming to Elsinore of a company of strolling actors, and some of these performers entered immediately afterwards.

Hamlet greeted them with "a kind of joy" and called upon one of them to recite the speech that he had formerly heard him deliver, in which Aeneas tells Dido about the fall of Troy; and, although the recitation was long, the Prince insisted on having the final portion given, which describes Hecuba's sorrow.

After a while, Hamlet very courteously dismissed

Gertrude of Denmark

Polonius and all except the chief among the actors. He asked this one to stage a drama for the evening of the next day. This play was entitled "The Murder of Gonzago," into which he proposed to insert a passage. The actor consented to give the performance according to Hamlet's desire. Then he took his leave of the Prince, and Rosencrantz and Guildenstern followed him.

Being at last entirely alone, Hamlet lapsed into soliloquy and berated himself as "A dull and muddy mettled rascal" because he had yet done nothing definite to avenge his father's murder. He passed from that mood to one, in which he admitted that he was troubled by a question whether the Ghost, whom he had seen, were really his father's spirit or were the devil who might be taking advantage of his own weakness and melancholy, to lead him to murder his innocent uncle. Then he remembered that he had heard,

"That guilty creatures sitting at a play
Have by the very cunning of the scene
Been struck so to the soul that presently
They have proclaimed their malefactions."

And he went on to say,

Gertrude of Denmark

"I'll have these players
Play something like the murder of my father
Before mine uncle.   I'll observe his looks;
I'll tent him to the quick; if he but blench
I know my course."

CHAPTER VI

CLAUDIUS had the more influence over Gertrude because he consulted her, and associated her with himself, in all possible ways. The elder and the worthier king, who had possessed her as a wife, had esteemed her intellect rather lightly. He had petted her, caressed her, said "I" to her, and sent her to stay in her boudoir while he discussed both family matters and statecraft with other counsellors.

But it was "we" with this man. Her name was so present in his mind that it rushed spontaneously to his lips. In moments of perplexity or of pain, his soul (such as it was) cried out for her. It was "Gertrude, Gertrude," "dear Gertrude," "sweet Gertrude," on whom he kept calling.

Her large consciousness of his constant appeal for her sympathy, and of his desire to know her thoughts, was an obstacle in the way of her seeing that there was any reserve in him towards her. She never guessed that his spirit turned desperately from the brink of a fathomless gulf of wicked secrecy, in an aching effort after consolation in superficial communion with her.

Just at this moment therefore, Gertrude became almost happy, even about Hamlet, because her husband seemed to be walking hand in hand with her, sharing a common sorrow and having a common purpose to search out the cause of her son's malady and to apply a cure to it.

Although she had hesitated to adopt the theory that love for Ophelia had jarred the working of Hamlet's brain, she gladly embraced it after a little reflection, embraced it thankfully indeed, because it relieved her own deep dread lest she herself had been the disturbing element in his mind. Moreover, she was fond of Ophelia, cared not a whit for the girl's inferior station, and was pleased to take part in a love affair.

Ophelia was sent for and, on entering the castle, was led to a chamber near the Queen's. After a little delay, Gertrude, all diamond sparkle as to jewelry, all opalescence as to personality, flashed into the girl's presence. Creamy laces floated around her head and shoulders. The diamonds glittered beneath and above the filmy meshes. Brilliance and softness, tender beauty and graceful movement,—these seemed to be the whole of her, till she spoke and laughed. Then she became incarnate music.

She gathered the motherless girl like a trembling blossom to her bosom. Ophelia, who did not know why she had been summoned, marvelled at this great condescension. It comforted her however, since although she knew nothing, she had nevertheless surmised that the order, to come to the Castle, might have something to do with the revelation, which her father had told her that he should make, and she had come in shuddering terror lest she were to encounter blame and condemnation.

When she was free to move, she fell upon her knees, and said timidly, "Madam, your kindness makes me hope that I have not offended your Majesty in any way."

The Queen laughed, dropped easily on an ottoman and bade Ophelia sit upon a low cushion beside her, put her arm around her and said, "Does the Prince love you, and do you care a little bit for him?"

Ophelia blushed. The Queen whispered, "I love each reddened spot on your white cheeks. They show you to be as sweet as untouched roses and as pure as lilies in an Angel's hand."

She smoothed Ophelia's golden hair, saying, "I give you a mother's blessing."

Then she told the plan, and babbled of her boy.

"He will be the King of Denmark some day," she said. "He will do wonderful things. Denmark will be greater because he will have lived in it. Mayhap he'll lead a crusade. Mayhap you'll go with him to the Holy Land."

She stopped, laughed again. "Isn't it odd!" she said. "He is thirty years old. We are going to marry him—to you, little Ophelia,—to *you*. He'll get well then. He'll be a great prince,—but today, I keep thinking what he did and how he looked when he was a baby. Such a beautiful baby! Oh, the darling things I can tell you about him! He whispered 'Mama' to me when he was but eight months old, though he spoke no other word, nor that again, for five months more. Now this errand you go upon, Ophelia, it is to look straight into his soul, as one who is ready to enter and dwell therein forever after. You are old enough to do it in good womanly fashion. Why, child of my heart, you are two months older than I was when the Prince was born." A pause, then a sudden breath which bore to Ophelia's ears, these words, "How the King kissed me when first he saw me after the babe had come!"

She checked her speech with a sigh, remembering that the day of her child's birth had been that of the

fatal duel between his father and the elder Fortinbras. Her pain had been flooded through with
horror and terror because of the destructive encounter, which she knew was occurring in that very
hour of her creative agony.

But she had never permitted herself to blame King
Hamlet, nor let herself feel that he had been inconsiderate of his young wife, when he arranged to
fight such a duel at just that time.

Pushing aside her memory of the past, Gertrude
discussed methods with Ophelia, and told her that
she thought it would be wise for her to use the simple
girlish trick and offer his presents back to Hamlet,
for surely, if he loved her, he would not take them
without taking her also. And then, Oh, then all
would be well!

"Don't be afraid because of his distemper," she
added. "He is always my gentle Hamlet just the
same."

She sent to Ophelia's home for the casket of
jewelry. When it had been brought, they both has-
tened to the appointed lobby, where they came into
the presence of Claudius, Polonius, Rosencrantz and
Guildenstern.

Ophelia stood deferentially apart. Gertrude
asked the young men whether her son had received

them well and whether they had assayed him to any pastime. Rosencrantz told her of Hamlet's desire to have a play enacted at the court that same night.

She was pleased to hear the King say cordially that he would attend the performance.

She was a little sorry that Claudius asked her to leave the room after the young men had withdrawn from the audience. She, however, recognized the validity of the King's statement, in support of his request for her departure, that he and Ophelia's father would be "lawful espials" of such a scene as the meeting between Hamlet and the girl, and so she submitted with her accustomed grace. But before going, she beckoned Ophelia to come near for a last word and a kiss. She said,

"For your part, Ophelia, I do wish
  That your good beauties be the happy cause
  Of Hamlet's wildness; so shall I hope your virtues
  Will bring him to his wonted way again,
  To both your honors."

Thus a great queen and a mother, out of her true heart, spoke to a low-born girl, and, up from the inner depths of a maiden's soul, fluttered the tremulous confession, "Madam, I wish it may."

CHAPTER VII

O PHELIA did not know where her father went
when he and the King left the lobby. She
had not heard much of the preceding dialogue; she
merely saw them all depart and leave her alone in
the great, high-studded hall.

She looked neither to the right nor to the left, nor
upward at all. Had she glanced up towards a bal-
cony, which overhung the lower floor, she would have
seen nothing. Claudius and her father were there
watching and listening, but they were too clever
to place themselves where it would have been
possible for anyone on the floor to catch a glimpse of
them. If afterwards, in their excitement, as some
actors represent them to have done, they did move
forward so that Hamlet saw them, Ophelia herself
did not look up and learn that they were there.

Ophelia sat down on a low bench and kept her eyes
fastened on a book which her father had given her.
Unconscious that he was near enough to rush to her
defense, should Hamlet's lunacy lead him to do anything violent, this sixteen year old child waited for

the coming of a madman. She had been asked to do a terrible thing,—to face incorporated insanity and to wrestle with it spiritually. She was frightened.

Hamlet came in. He walked up and down the hall, his lips moving as though he were talking to himself. Back and forth he went, passing her several times without seeing her. She glanced at him furtively now and then.

His dress was a little less slovenly than it had been when he appeared before her in her closet. He was nevertheless sufficiently en dishabille to justify the characterization of the change in him, as "transformation," which Claudius had once given, supported by the explanation to Rosencrantz and Guildenstern, that "nor the exterior nor the inward man resembles that it was."

Shakspeare must have intended to show Hamlet in this disarray to the public audience, as well as to Ophelia in her closet, since Anthony Scoloker, who had seen the play on the stage, wrote in 1603 or 1604, of the action of the mad Diaphantus in some other drama

"Puts off his clothes; his shirt he only wears,
Much like mad Hamlet."

Modern actors, ignoring the special significance,

as to real or imitated insanity, of scanty and disordered dress, and not being obliged by the text to represent Hamlet, as he appeared in Ophelia's closet, cut out the whole clothing business and dress him in nice black velvet whenever he is seen on the stage.

Soiled, shabby and somewhat torn of raiment, the Prince of Denmark, there in Elsinore, continued his march and kept up the moving pantomime of his lips. Now and then, he articulated a disjointed word or two: "Mortal coil"—"weary life," "conscience does make cowards of us all."

Ophelia distinguished these phrases. A few other vocal sounds did not come clearly to her ears. She heard his step upon the floor, regular and slow. To all this noise her heart kept beating an echo of increasing terror.

Suddenly he saw her,—paused an instant, and then approaching, he greeted her deferentially.

She rose, moved towards him, and, kneeling, spoke words which stumbled a little on her palpitating breath,

"Good my lord,
How does your honour for this many a day?"

He raised her and made a proper answer.

[83]

Then with increasing fright, she began her allotted part in the drama that had been arranged;

> "My lord, I have remembrances of yours,
> That I have long'd long to re-deliver;
> I pray you, now receive them."

Thus she staked her life on the chance of a gracious answer.

"No, not I," said Hamlet, "I never gave you aught."

She tried again, and the shock of the verbal blow, which he had dealt her, imparted a little added insistence to her manner and nerved her to a higher courage in her own defense.

Taking the necklaces and other trinkets from the casket, she said;

> "My honour'd lord, I know right well you did;
> And with them words of so sweet breath compos'd
> As made the things more rich."

She looked straight at him. For two months, she had been shut away from him as in a cloister, and, all the while, she had been revolving the thought that he might have sought her ruin. Now she held out to him the jewels he had bestowed upon her—were they the price he had offered for her chastity?

"Take these again;" she said with piteous dignity,

"for to the noble mind
Rich gifts wax poor, when givers prove unkind.
There, my lord."

Did he guess her meaning? As she stood before
him speaking out of the gulf of maidenly agony into
which he had plunged her, did he realize, in the
least, how unkind he had been? Did he get any
sight of the road to heaven which she was offering to
his repentance?

He turned upon her with the question, which addressed to a woman is always an insult, if it be not
prompted by the certain knowledge, which alone permits such a reference.

"Ha, ha!" he shrugged his shoulders, "Are you
honest?"

"My lord?" and the jewels fell unheeded to the
floor.

"Are you fair?" he persisted.

"What means your lordship?" she asked, and held
her head up once again.

Then he did the unspeakable thing, giving her the
sort of counsel which no man, not a near kinsman,
can give to a virtuous woman without its becoming
an indignity, "If you be honest and fair, your

honesty should admit no discourse to your beauty."

She struggled still to maintain the erect carriage of her innocent soul. "Could beauty, my lord," she made answer, "have better commerce than with honesty?"

His reply to this, though somewhat academic in its unnecessary attempt to deal out argument, still fell lower than decency in its verbiage. He stabbed with words of hateful insinuation. Then he seemed to retreat a little from his own thrust and muttered, "I did love you once."

To which came her responding whisper, "Indeed, my lord, you made me believe so."

This went farther than he intended towards an issue which might have imposed some obligation upon him, and he speedily cut the knot of his entanglement with this girl, by a blunt denial of what he had already affirmed. "I loved you not," he declared.

That finished the unrighteous business which he was prosecuting.

She made out to say, "I was the more deceived."

After that, she was simply a young thing which, having received a mortal wound, has not yet died.

Did Hamlet suppose that Ophelia had, during the past months, denied him access to her society be-

cause she did not love him? And might he therefore be somewhat excused for the brutal treatment
which he accorded her in this scene? Who can say?
Is it possible that he knew so little of custom or of
natural feeling, as not to realize that he had only to
offer the wedding ring to be acquitted by her of un-
kindness? even though he should learn afterwards
that "the main voice of Denmark" would prevent
his marrying her.

However it may be as to Hamlet's inner prompting for his cruel speeches, after that moan, "I was
the more deceived," although she was death-stricken
and, as it fell out, worse than death-stricken, the out-
flowing current of her being became one undiluted
stream of love. She had no more thought of self-
assertion and no more words with which to utter such
a thought.

She drifted slowly backward from him and seated
herself on the bench. He stepped past the jewels on
the floor and stood over her, continuing his reckless
harangue. She distinguished but few of the words
he spoke. His voice was sometimes stormy, sometimes soft and almost tender, but nearly all he said
sounded to her irrelevant and confused. Why was
he bidding her go to a nunnery? Of what was he
accusing himself? What was all this about "arrant

knaves" and "crawling between earth and heaven?"

Suddenly a sharp question cut across the verbal torrent. "Where's your father?"

She did not know, and at the moment she did not even remember that she did not know. She answered, "At home, my lord."

She dizzily heard the Prince say, "Let the doors be shut upon him, that he may play the fool nowhere but in's own house."

Afterwards, the fact that Hamlet had called her father a fool seemed stamped into the substance of her brain, but just then she realized the word only as one of the many incoherencies and contradictions in his speech which indicated his insanity, and her accustomed prayer repeated itself within her, "O, help him, you sweet heavens!"

His words pelted on, "if thou wilt needs marry, marry a fool;"—down, down upon her from his beautiful lips the terrible words kept falling.

"O heavenly powers restore him," her silent prayer kept winging its way upward.

Again descended upon her and surrounded her a windy blast of epithets . . . and then Hamlet left her . . . and the jewels still lay upon the floor.

After a while, the feelings of love and grief, that were filling her whole being, began to be more definite; and Shakspeare has translated her sighs into words:

"O, what a noble mind is here o'erthrown!   .
  The courtier's, scholar's, soldier's; eye, tongue, sword;
  The expectancy and rose of the fair state,
  The glass of fashion and the mould of form,
  The observ'd of all observers, quite, quite down!
  And I, of ladies most deject and wretched,
  That suck'd the honey of his music vows,
  Now see that noble and most sovereign reason,
  Like sweet bells jangled out of tune, and harsh;
  That unmatch'd form and feature of blown youth
  Blasted with ecstasy: O, woe is me,
  To have seen what I have seen, see what I see!"

The King and Polonius came into the lobby talking together. The shrewd, clear intellect of Claudius had brought him to a swift decision anent his nephew.

"Love!" he was saying, "his affections do not that way tend; nor what he spake, though it lack'd form a little, was not like madness. There's something in his soul o'er which his melancholy sits on brood, and I do doubt the hatch and the disclose will be some danger; which for to prevent, I have in quick determination thus set it down: he shall with speed to England, for the demand of our neglected tribute."

Claudius, this same afternoon, summarized to Gertrude his opinion of Hamlet's mental and moral condition in fashion not wholly unlike his speech to Polonius on the subject. He said:

"We must learn the exact nature of his fancies if indeed he be insane. Madness in a prince might easily lead the imaginative multitude into riotous behavior. If he be sane the issue may be even worse, for he is certainly coddling some unhappy thought in his breast. And this fact, perceived and only half understood, might stir some spirit of discontent which would lead to civil war. He is not acting like a loyal son to you and myself. Perhaps he is out of temper because he lost the election to the throne."

"Oh," she pleaded. "Be not offended with him for feeling that."

Claudius failed to smile as he usually did in response to any appeal from her.

He answered gravely, "See him yourself after the play is over tonight. Get at the inmost heart of him and gather for me the very truth."

He shuddered a little, stood silent a moment, and then with an effect of effort in every movement he leaned resolutely down and kissed her.

Then he told her of his plan to send Hamlet on an embassy to England. She was grateful. She thought that her son was to be entrusted with the performance of high and honorable business, and that it was fine in Claudius thus to recognize Hamlet's ability and so to give him opportunity to show it. She felt it proved that the King thought Hamlet's malady was but a temporary and superficial matter; and she was glad for that.

Claudius said nothing whatever to her about the love affair with Ophelia, and, noting his silence, she also made no reference to it.

She thought his silence was due to delicacy of feeling, and for that also she was grateful. She did not want to talk with anybody just then about Ophelia.

A few minutes after the King, Polonius, and Ophelia had all left the lobby, Gertrude had met the girl staggering alone through one of the corridors; and had asked her, "What did the Prince say?"

"Madam," Ophelia had answered, "My lord Hamlet has strange thoughts. He did seem to have forgotten much that he had said or written to me. He bade me become a nun. I beg your Majesty let me go home to my father's house till evening. I am tired."

"Oh God help you, child," cried Gertrude softly, and let her go, but sent one of her own waiting women with her.

CHAPTER VIII

THE evening, after this interview with Ophelia, was the one for which Hamlet had staged the ordeal of a play to represent a murder like to that, which the Ghost had told him Claudius had committed. It was to be enacted before the uneasy King, the unsuspecting Gertrude and the intimate members of the court circle.

While the players were making ready for the performance, Hamlet held discourse with Horatio and expressed his affection for him, and his trust in his judgment and character, in what was very beautiful and evidently sincere phrase:

"Horatio, thou art e'en as just a man
   As e'er my conversation cop'd withal.

                . . . Dost thou hear?
Since my dear soul was mistress of her choice,
And could of men, distinguish, her election
Hath seal'd thee for herself; for thou hast been
As one, in suffering all, that suffers nothing,
A man that fortune's buffets and rewards
Hath ta'en with equal thanks and blest are those

Whose blood and judgment are so well commingled
That they are not a pipe for Fortune's finger
To sound what stop she please. Give me that man
That is not passion's slave, and I will wear him,
In my heart's core; ay, in my heart of hearts,
As I do thee."

Before this evening, Hamlet had revealed to his
friend all the main features of his own interview with
the Ghost. Horatio was also acquainted with Hamlet's fear that his suspicion of Claudius might be un-
just. Hamlet now told him,

"There is a play to-night before the king;
One scene of it comes near the circumstance
Which I have told thee of my father's death,
I prithee, when thou seest that act afoot,
Even with the very comment of thy soul
Observe mine uncle; if his occulted guilt
Do not itself unkennel in one speech,
It is a damned ghost that we have seen,
And my imaginations are as foul
As Vulcan's stithy. Give him heedful note:
For I mine eyes will rivet to his face,
And after we will both our judgments join
In censure of his seeming."

Gertrude of Denmark

Horatio promised to give full attention; and after this grave and noble converse with his friend, Hamlet left him and entered that portion of the hall, which was especially reserved for royalty and its closer circle of attendance.

At the appointed hour Ophelia came in and took her place.

Gertrude swept in afterwards to the sound of music. She held her head high as she walked beside the King, herself what, barring a few weeks, she had been for thirty years, a wife, a queen and the mother of the first Prince in the realm. She sat down with a movement of controlled dignity, and yet swaying a little, as if to the outward music of the orchestra and the inward rhythm of royal life. She threw her gracious smile around the whole immediate group, so that each person received it as a particular and special greeting.

Then she sent a more intent and searching gaze here and there. In a moment, her expression changed. She had seen her heart's desire. But the King engaged Hamlet at once in a brief colloquy, so that his mother could not draw his attention to herself. And the Prince next turned, of his own accord, to Polonius and skillfully made occasion for a rude and insulting remark in reply to the old man's answer to a question.

The coming of the actors was announced, and then Gertrude got her chance to speak. She had the sort of voice upon which the listener's spirit floats. She leaned a little forward and said: "Come hither, my dear Hamlet, sit by me."

He flung himself at Ophelia's feet with flippant reply: "No, good mother, here's metal more attractive."

Gertrude did, what millions of other mothers have done, and millions more are likely to do. Hearing his refusal of her request, she serenely acquiesced in the order of nature, and bade herself be glad that he wanted to be with Ophelia. Yet need he have worded his refusal in just that way, there before the whole court?

She turned with a friendly glance to Claudius and enveloped him with her gracious and interested manner as in a shimmering mantle.

Probably Hamlet noticed his mother's peculiar graciousness towards his uncle, and it irritated him. At any rate, he called Ophelia's attention to her, saying, "Look you how cheerfully my mother looks, and my father died within's two hours."

The silliness of this assertion served only to remind the bewildered girl that it was a lunatic who was sitting at her feet. Hoping to recall him to his senses, she answered: "Nay, 'tis twice two months, my lord."

He accepted her assertion without contradiction, and thus it is made certain to the reader, that it was at least nine or ten weeks after his interview with the Ghost when, a day or two previously, he had made his intrusion into her closet.

Absorbed in each other, Claudius and Gertrude paid little attention to the talk and movement around them, till they were startled by hearing Hamlet shout his burlesque epitaph, "For, O, for, O, the hobbyhorse is forgot!"

Gertrude looked frightened for an instant. Quickly though, the stronger fear that the courtiers would notice her fright, arose and strangled the other. She changed her position and made it evident that she was watching a "dumb-show" performance on the stage. She perceived that, therein, the story was being briefly suggested, which was later to be presented by both speech and action in the regular play.

Gertrude, watching this pantomime, saw a mimic king and queen moving about in a garden, and making loving gestures as they talked to each other. The

action is thus described, "The [player] queen kneels
and makes show of protestation unto him [the player
king]. He takes her up and declines his head upon
her neck; lays him down upon a bank of flowers:
she, seeing him asleep, leaves him."

There was nothing in all this to disturb Gertrude.
The pantomime continued. "Anon comes in a fellow, takes off his [the player king's] crown and
kisses it." At that sight, Gertrude whispered to
Claudius, "A good wife would have taken the thing
off herself; it would make his neck lame to lie there
with it on."

She laughed merrily. Claudius was silent. She
did not notice that the man in the garden kissed the
crown. No chord vibrated uneasily within her, because the dumb interloper poured something in the
sleeper's ears, and fled. Nor did any recognizing
sense move her when it became apparent that the
drops had been poisonous. But Gertrude trembled
with sympathy when she beheld the agonized movements of the wife who, returning to the scene, found
her husband dead.

The stage poisoner began to make love to the
widow. This was repulsive to Gertrude because of
its inherent horribleness, and she was disgusted with

the woman's final acceptance of that outrageous wooing.

Such was the sum total of the effect upon Gertrude made by this piece of mimicry. There was nothing in it all, except that it happened in a garden, to remind her of her own experience on the day that King Hamlet died. She had not been with him when he had lain down for what proved to be his last sleep. She had been spending some hours at the nearest convent and, although hastily summoned, she did not arrive home until after the body had been removed to one of the castle halls. At her first sight of it, she had beheld Claudius kneeling beside it, his face hidden, and his whole body shaken with sobs. They were not make believe sobs either. He had lifted a tear-stained countenance to her.

The spoken play began, and for a while Gertrude only half listened to it. She was watching her son, and her dominant thought was, "Oh, how hopelessly mad he is!"

When the player queen said,

"In second husband let me be accurst!
None wed the second but who killed the first!"

instead of finding the speech "wormwood," as Hamlet was supposing that she did, Gertrude merely thought rather triumphantly, perhaps a little self-righteously, how lacking the writer of that drama was in knowledge of the tender and unselfish motives which move many women to contract second marriages.

The next speech made by the player queen aroused in Gertrude's heart a definite feeling of antagonism, because it seemed to her practically to deny the validity of the marriage sacrament, which she believed consecrated every such union, were it first or second, and whether formed for love or not. Neither of her own marriages had really been contracted because of love on her part, although affection very like to love, had developed in the first, and maternal passion had dictated the second, while a capacity to feel amiable tenderness had reconciled her to both, and her creed had made them equally sacred to her.

She listened with tolerant sympathy to the speech of the garrulous player king, beginning

"I do believe you think what now you speak,
But what we do determine oft we break."

His orderly analysis of the way that resolutions wither in the atmosphere of new emergencies, and under the stimulus of new necessities, appealed to Gertrude. She remembered with no accompaniment of unpleasant feeling, that, often during King Hamlet's lifetime, she had thought that, should she survive him, she would never marry again; and she said now to herself, "I was young and did not know in what proportion the elements in life are mixed."

Her son's voice broke in upon her musings, "Madam, how like you the play?"

She made an answer which was the natural sequence to the thoughts she had been formulating: "The lady protests too much, methinks."

She spoke low, but Hamlet shouted his reply, "O, but she'll keep her word."

Then Gertrude shivered, perceiving, rather indignantly, that his tone implied an attack upon herself. "The poor mad wretch," she thought, "he does not dream that it was for his sake I married." Then an angrier feeling than she often had swept over her. It was instantly softened however by maternal pity, and was even touched with maternal amusement; "Stupid child!" she murmured below her breath, "Why can't he divine why I married his uncle? Must he be told everything and have the words spelled to him, ere he can understand?"

Gertrude of Denmark

All this while Hamlet had been reclining on cushions at Ophelia's feet, with his head in her lap, an attitude which the customs of the period permitted. Gertrude, looking intently, saw that Ophelia's face was white and her eyes were wild with agony, and that she often turned away from gazing at that head upon her knees.

Ophelia knew nothing of Hamlet's special interest in the purport of the play. She knew nothing of the Ghost. She knew none of his fancies about his mother. She had absolute knowledge only of the Queen's whisper to her that very noon time, that love and marriage to the Prince might be hers if, for such prizes, she would struggle with a monstrous shape of madness, overcome it by her own pure beauty, and, as it were, sign its brow with the cross, thereby restoring this figure of horror to the likeness of her loved one. She had dared the contest and had been herself defeated.

It was now scarcely six hours since Hamlet had called her father a fool, had denied that he had meant the love he had professed for her, had bade her either "marry a fool" or enter a nunnery, and had reviled her as one of the women who paint, who "jig," who "amble" and who affect an innocent ignorance as a mask for their wantonness.

Gertrude of Denmark

Only the pulsing minutes of six hours before . . .
and now he lay there with his beautiful head on her
knee. His voice low and melodious, coming to her
ears. . . . And what was he whispering? . . . He
put up his hand and pushed back his curls from his
forehead. He was very near her. . . . She had offered him her virtuous love so little while before!
. . . What was he saying now?

Innocent and ignorant she was, as it was possible
for a girl to be, who lived in her environment of
speech and song—and more virtuous, as befitted the
nobility of her soul, than she was ignorant; but she
could not fail to understand the tenor of his words.
He was pouring into her hearing indelicacy after
indelicacy, allusion after allusion, and they all concerned herself. . . . They were not merely general
phrases.

They were so pertinent and so personal—and his
hair all the while tumbling on her knees,—that she
trembled. Her very soul trembled. She was wholly
in his power. She tried in vain to make him talk
of other things. She could not withdraw from his
presence, and his personality held her thoughts. He
showed her no mercy. His magnetism, the mere
reading of which has bewitched the world for centuries, subdued her.

He did this awful thing to a helpless girl, between times of watching Claudius and his mother with the eyes of a lynx. He committed a spiritual rape in that hour, apparently as a momentary relaxation from the serious business of a detective which he had in hand.

Moreover he was concerned in a bigger enterprise than even that of a detective. He had staged that play in order to judge, by its results, whether the apparition, which he had seen, were his dead father's spirit or were the Devil himself in masquerade. So far as a human being could do so, he had summoned Heaven and Hell to yield up to him their uttermost secrets, and, while waiting for this dread revelation, he tortured and sought to debase the mind of the girl whom he had made to love him.

The murder scene in the spoken play did make Gertrude writhe inwardly. She did not like to see murders performed either in real life or on the stage.

At last, she heard Claudius breathing heavily at her side. Suddenly he rose staggering to his feet. Ophelia gave a little cry. There was some tumultuous movement and noise in the circle immediately close to the royal party. Hamlet's voice, triumphant and bitter, cut through it all to his mother's ears.

Gertrude saw his marvellous eyes glaring at her husband, as he yelled, "What, frighted with false fire!"

She gave no thought to his possible meaning. She caught Claudius by the hand.

"How fares my lord?" she whispered.

The play stopped. Torches were brought, seats pushed back. Cries rang here and there. Hurriedly the actors disappeared from the stage. Polonius took charge of the dispersion of the audience. Some went out with the King and Queen in more or less orderly arrangement, while others lingered in confused groups and some straggled more slowly into the corridors. And everybody wondered mentally and some openly, as to what the trouble was all about, and queried whether the King would die of the stroke, that most of them supposed he must have had.

The Queen was at her husband's side when, in a passageway, she saw Ophelia among the attendants who were clustered there. The girl's cheeks were white, but her eyes were burning with a fear more terrible than should ever be seen in the eyes of a maiden.

When the tumult had ebbed out of the hall, Hamlet and Horatio stood staring at each other, alone together close to the stage from which the players had fled in bewilderment and terror.

Hamlet threw up his arms and began to sing,

"Why let the strucken deer go weep,
The hart ungalled play;
For some must watch, while some must sleep:
So runs the world away."

He made a few speeches of jesting mockery, and then drew a long sighing breath, and said more quietly,

"O good Horatio, I'll take the Ghost's word for a thousand pound. Did'st perceive?"

"Very well, my lord," answered Horatio in a toneless voice of complete admission.

Hamlet persisted, in order to make sure that Horatio meant to give a full endorsement of his own present belief in his uncle's guilt.

"Upon the talk of the poisoning?" he asked.

"I did very well note him," replied Horatio.

There could be no further doubt in either man's mind. Each one's opinion supported the other's. Hamlet relapsed again into wild and farcical utterance.

Rosencrantz and Guildenstern came into the hall

bringing a message that the Queen desired to speak with her son in her closet.

"We shall obey," said Hamlet, "were she ten times our mother."

Claudius did have an attack of vertigo, but he wanted to recover from it so much that he succeeded so far as to be able to insist on Gertrude's going very soon to her own room to meet her son.

She left the King sitting half collapsed in his chair. He remained motionless for some minutes. He knew that he was playing a desperate game. But he was not yet sure that the odds were too heavy against him.

The scene in the theatre had at first overcome him only emotionally. Now, he was growing aware that Hamlet probably had some design in causing that particular play to be represented.

Yet, he asked himself, was that possible? His crime had been so carefully contrived and executed, that he was unable to imagine how Hamlet could have got any idea that he had committed it. He had heard of similar murders committed in a similar way. Was it not more likely that the plot of this play had been founded on some such known incident, and its representation in his presence had been the work of chance, than that—; when Claudius had got so far in his musings, he stopped, shivered, and did not go on putting his further thought into definite though unspoken words.

But what was he doing and daring in sending Hamlet's mother, his wife, Gertrude, to pluck the secret from her son's heart?

The plan for such an interview had been formed before the play had made such terrifying revelation to Claudius of the possible nature of Hamlet's hidden thought. Polonius had suggested it. Polonius was coming in a few minutes to hold a last conversation with the King before Hamlet was to meet his mother. Claudius felt afraid to tell Polonius to prevent the interview from occurring, afraid to seem in the old man's eyes afraid of what might happen in that interview.

Still, the horror of sending Gertrude to make such a discovery as she might make—that her son suspected her husband of having murdered the dead King, his own brother, her former husband!

What would happen if she did learn that Hamlet suspected such a thing?

Then, in a great access of feeling, Claudius knew that he was less afraid to let Gertrude look, if need were, into the blackest depth of Hamlet's heart, than he was to prevent her going.

And,—here he smiled grimly,—whatever she learned in this awful coming interview, at least, he himself would henceforth know just what was the monstrous shape of danger with which he must grapple.

Then suddenly, incongruously, Claudius remembered that there was a Heaven to which men prayed.

He was, however, obliged to see Rosencrantz and Guildenstern as well as Polonius before he could be left alone long enough to consider that memory.

CHAPTER IX

CLAUDIUS held his interview with Rosencrantz and Guildenstern, telling them to prepare to start at once for England in attendance upon Hamlet. But neither then, nor afterwards when he did mention a sealed order, did he utter any hint to them that the English authorities were to be requested to put Hamlet to death.

So far as there is available evidence on the subject, these young men were entirely innocent of any connivance at, or acquiescence in, any plot against Hamlet's life.

The most ingenious and unscrupulous prosecuting attorney, in the world, would hardly be able, before a jury, to manufacture evidence that would incriminate a prisoner on trial, out of such flimsy verbal stuff as the Rev. C. E. Moberley uses in his effort to besmirch the characters of these school-fellows of the Prince of Denmark. This clerical gentleman notes the fact that, in Shakspeare's rendition of the story, Claudius in this interview said,

Gertrude of Denmark

"I like him not, nor stands it safe with us
To let his madness range. Therefore prepare you;
I your commission will forthwith despatch,
And he to England shall along with you.
The terms of our estate may not endure
Hazard so near us as doth hourly grow
Out of his lunacies."

The young men made natural and loyal answers
to their sovereign, whom it was their duty to protect
and to obey. All that they expressed is summed
sufficiently, in a few words spoken by Guildenstern,
in reply to his king,

"We will ourselves provide;
Most holy and religious fear it is
To keep those many, many bodies safe
That live and feed upon your majesty."

The reverend critic draws a conclusion, from the
King's mention of "your commission" and the answer of his envoys, which he puts into the following
sentence: "Rosencrantz and Guildenstern are *there-*
fore privy to the traitorous scheme for killing
Hamlet in England." (The italics are the present
chronicler's.)

Heaven save the mark! Does the clergyman think

Claudius was such an imbecile as to have unbosomed himself to that extent even had he then formed the scheme? It is extremely probable that he had not fully decided upon it at this time. But if he had, in what dictionary can a definition be found of the words employed which would necessarily reveal such a plot, if there were one? That these attachés, of the proposed embassy to England, consented to take a sealed document with them no more implies knowledge of its contents than the mention of chops and tomato sauce, in Pickwick's letter to a woman, implied a promise to marry her. But Mr. Moberley has presented himself, as a competitor in absurdity, to the prosecuting attorney, in the famous suit against Samuel Pickwick for breach of promise.

It is only fair to conclude that, on this fateful night in Elsinore, Rosencrantz and Guildenstern were acting with good faith, in the character of guardians chosen, by the Prince's nearest kindred, to watch over his safety, and to take him where he could harm nobody and nobody would have any desire to harm him. They were the mediaeval substitutes for the modern alienist and the modern nurse, and to give a proper stamp to their whole task, it was connected with a diplomatic errand of importance to the realm

Gertrude of Denmark

of Denmark. Who can conjecture their thoughts when they themselves met the great surprise of unmerited and unrighteously procured death in England!

After these ill-fated lads had obediently left the royal presence, Claudius received Polonius who told him that Hamlet was going to see his mother, and added that he would station himself where, though unseen, he could hear whatever passed between the queen and her son.

Left at last alone in the midnight, Claudius gave himself up to self analysis. In this, he showed a complete understanding of the nature of sin and its relation to the moral law. He turned upon the whole subject the force of a very strong and subtle intellect. He attempted no self deception. He knew what he had done and why he had done it. He correctly analyzed and defined his crime, and stated the truth thereof to Heaven.

He held to the belief that, by repentance, he might cleanse the hand which was red with a brother's blood.

He wanted to repent because he did so believe, that is, he wanted to repent in order to save himself from any direful consequences of his guilt, and not because he wanted to save other people from pain and sorrow as a result of what he had done.

He was too clearly intellectual not to perceive the moral flaw in his desire. Still he tried to get up a feeling which might help him to obtain some sort of mercy from "the sweet heavens."

He essayed the utterance of the formula, "Forgive me my foul murther." He recoiled, in agonized certainty, from the futile fancy that such repetition would adequately provide for his great need.

Inexorable to himself as an accredited judge might have been, he groaned,

"That cannot be; since I am still possess'd
Of those effects for which I did the murther,
My crown, mine own ambition, and my queen.
May one be pardon'd and retain the offence?"

Claudius knew that he was not prepared to relinquish those things in order to gain which he had committed murder.

Here, however, is a plain statement of what he had gained that he did not possess while King Hamlet was living, namely, the crown, ambition, and the Queen. Ambition is an intangible "effect." Claudius had always possessed ambition, but here the word undoubtedly carries the meaning, not only of purpose but also, of immediate opportunity to carry out a purpose.

Still whatever haze may obscure the question as to the especial significance which the word "ambition" bore in his mind just then, the words "crown" and "queen" denote definite realities. No matter what the Ghost half imagined, or Hamlet believed, or what opinion all the critics have developed since the Great Wizard wrote the story, Claudius knew, and in this moment proclaimed before Heaven, that he had not possessed his brother's wife while that brother was alive.

Let the wraith of Gertrude of Denmark henceforth down the ages in peace. Out of the mouth of the criminal himself has issued her vindication. And the verdict is,—Not Guilty.

It was only because she was wholly guiltless of any sin whatsoever, that Claudius had dared to let her probe Hamlet's mind and heart. He felt that she was too good herself to believe in anybody's capacity for such crime as he, Claudius, had committed. If Hamlet should suggest any such suspicion to her, she would think either that the conjecture had been born of insanity or had been accepted by his ill-judging mind on inadequate evidence.

Hamlet coming in, unseen by Claudius, and surprising him praying on his knees, made some remarks to his own heart about his dead father, which contrast curiously with that description of him as Hyperion, Jove, Mars, Mercury and everything "wholesome," which he gave a few minutes later to his mother.

Staring at his kneeling uncle, whom he supposed to be feeling true repentance, he muttered,

"He took my father grossly; full of bread,
With all his crimes broad blown, as flush as May;
And how his audit stands, who knows save heaven?
But in our circumstance and course of thought,
'Tis heavy with him."

Making these bitter reflections, Hamlet stood motionless in a corner of the room; and, his presence unsuspected by his uncle, he glared at the figure kneeling before a crucifix, which was suspended against the wall of the alcove wherein the King knelt. Two candles, in sconces beside the crucifix, lighted the recess sufficiently.

Hamlet held a naked sword. A large candle

burned in a protruding brass holder fastened to a wall socket above his head. There was a strip of darkness in the chamber before him, but beyond that, a wide well-lighted space stretched in front of the alcove where Claudius crouched upon the floor. He did seem to crouch rather than to kneel there.

The King's head was uncovered. He wore a close-fitting jacket of richly scarlet velvet. Its surface gleamed in the candle-light. His blonde hair fell a little way down his back in heavy curls. His shoulders were slightly hunched and curved in unbeautiful lines. He was not actually deformed, but his body was not well shaped.

Hamlet noted this peculiarity of appearance as he stood, with the hilt of the rapier clenched in his fingers. He knew the exact spot where he must drive the blade through the velvet covering and through the solid flesh, in order to do the deadly work, to perform which he had made his secret entrance to the room.

His father had been fully six inches taller than his uncle, and yet Claudius was of the middle height of manhood, but he had some internal difficulty which had made him inapt at wrestling and unable to be a fast runner. King Hamlet could take creditable part in many athletic sports at which Claudius was unskilled. Such ability had been due to his possession of the "natural gifts," in which, even as a ghost, the older Hamlet had complacently remembered that his brother had been "poor."

The younger Hamlet, now standing there, watching his uncle kneel apparently in prayer, found some odd memories coming back to him. When he was a child, he had often heard his father mock at Claudius a little for his athletic failures and tease him about his lack of height.

"This boy of mine," King Hamlet had said, "will soon be so tall that he can give his cast-off garments to you, Sir Knight of Dwarfshire."

Perhaps King Hamlet did not guess how Claudius felt, when he heard such speeches tumble out on half contemptuous, half good-natured laughter from the handsome royal lips.

The boy Hamlet, with the uncomprehending, almost innocent cruelty of childhood, had delighted in his father's taunting raillery. Claudius had sometimes sullenly and silently hated both of his tormentors and had, sometimes, sullenly and silently, but honestly, tried not to hate either of them.

The man Hamlet, in this midnight hour, looked at the crouching figure and hated it unreservedly.

Gertrude of Denmark

A purpose came, vaguely at first, into his mind.
These were the words in which he gave it substance
and form:

"Now might I do it pat, now he is praying;
And now I'll do't.—And so he goes to heaven;
And so am I reveng'd.   That would be scanned:
A villain kills my father; and for that,
I, his sole son, do this same villain send
To heaven.
O, this is hire and salary, not revenge.
    * * * And am I then reveng'd,
To take him in the purging of his soul,
When he is fit and season'd for his passage?
No!
Up, sword, and know thou a more horrid hent:
When he is drunk asleep, or in his rage,
Or in the incestuous pleasure of his bed;
At gaming, swearing, or about some act
That has no relish of salvation in't;
Then trip him, that his heels may kick at heaven,
And that his soul may be as damn'd and black
As hell, whereto it goes."

The Prince made, with his own shoulders, a shrug-
ging gesture of satisfaction; said to himself, "My
mother stays";—threw his hand out towards the si-

lent figure of the murderer, hurled another thought at it,

"This physic but prolongs thy sickly days,"

and with noiseless step retreated from the room.

Claudius remained a brief while longer squatting in the alcove, his head nearly sunken on the floor in front of his body.

Finally he rose, stretching himself with a slow movement, betokening muscular difficulty and even physical pain. He stood erect a moment. He looked rather dazed. His lips dropped helplessly apart.

There was an expression of idiotic horror spread over his face.

He had failed to get Heaven on his side . . . and he knew it.

His glance grew firmer. He looked at the stone floor and he began to measure with his eyes the distance to the nearest window.

He calculated carefully, one . . . two . . . three paces. He stepped forward to prove his estimate— his gaze steady,—but his face otherwise vacant of expression. Four . . . five . . . six paces. He lost count, twice retreated and began again.

Suddenly he heard the whistling cry of a night-bird flying past an open window. He screeched, stopped in his walk, but went on counting. Seven . . . eight . . . he attempted to move again, stumbled and fell prone like an animal on all fours.

A sound issued mechanically from his lips, "Forgive me my foul murther."

Hearing his own voice as though it were another's, he recognized the purport of the words he had uttered. After a moment of utter silence in the room, he spoke low, her name, "Gertrude."

Then he flattened his hands upon the floor and with a scrambling effort, lifted himself from the beast-like posture into which he had fallen.

He stood up, said "Gertrude" again, and walked to the doorway.

Two hours later Claudius had begun to feel that Heaven had been very hard on him in forcing him to employ his own resources in self defence.

He did not really think that Heaven was to blame. He knew better. But he felt that way.

He felt that he had given Heaven a chance, by

performing a miracle, to make him good and worthy
of safety on this earth . . . And Heaven had not
cared enough, either about his being good or his being safe, to do it.

Hamlet went to seek his mother, having, a half
hour earlier in the evening, determined that in no
case whatever would he kill her. The words, in
which he had expressed that resolution, show that
he had been haunted, if not by an actual temptation,
still by the persistent thought that in some angry moment he might take her life.

After he had finished some dialogue, first with
Rosencrantz and Guildenstern and then with Polonius, which had been wild and indignant mockery on
his side, he had said to himself,

" 'Tis now the very witching time of night,
  When churchyards yawn, and hell itself breathes out
  Contagion to this world; now could I drink hot
      blood,
  And do such bitter business as the day
  Would quake to look on.   Soft! now to my mother.
  O heart, lose not thy nature; let not ever
  The soul of Nero enter this firm bosom;
  Let me be cruel, not unnatural.

Gertrude of Denmark

I will speak daggers to her, but use none;
My tongue and soul in this be hypocrites:
How in my words soever she be shent,
To give them seals never, my soul, consent!"

CHAPTER X

POLONIUS went to the Queen's room and told her that Hamlet was on his way to see her. She readily permitted the old man to conceal himself behind the arras, being indeed glad to have him thus close at hand, for she was alarmed at the idea of holding a lonely midnight interview with a madman, even though that madman were her own child. Yet she wanted to get that child into her presence, for she had all the inconsequent and conflicting emotions, which are apt to assail one in relation to some experiences.

Had Gertrude's life contained guilty secrets, she would have been afraid to permit Polonius to remain within hearing distance, during the coming interview, lest Hamlet should accuse her. She knew that her son was displeased by her "o'er hasty marriage." She had admitted to Claudius that she feared that such was the case. She had tried to think that the disturbance in Hamlet's mind was due only or chiefly to something about Ophelia, but she had been but half convinced and the events of the day had shaken that half conviction. Only complete innocence of any more serious fault, on her own part, than that of the hasty marriage, could have rendered her willing to accept in this terror-filled midnight hour, the presence of Polonius unseen by Hamlet and therefore unconstraining of any impulse towards accusing speech, which might seize her frantic son.

The Great Wizard must have gloried in the opportunity, given him by Gertrude's behavior, to show how a falsely suspected and high bred woman would act, if she did not even know that she was suspected.

Gertrude fully believed that Hamlet was insane, and nevertheless she felt that were he with her so that she could put her arms around his neck, and lay her head against his breast, he would somehow cease at once to be insane. Still while thinking and feeling, thus, she knew that should he enter the room where she sat alone, she would be afraid to go up to him and put her arms around his neck.

When at last Hamlet did come, Gertrude, like most persons who try to deal with the mystery of another's insanity, was entirely unable to speak to him with the tact of the wise physician who would control or soothe away delirium.

Her first words were so inappropriate to Hamlet's mood, whether he were sane or insane, that they prove her own innocence and her ignorance of Claudius' guilt. Nevertheless, her innocent speech was dynamite cast into her son's brain.

She said, "Hamlet, thou hast thy father much offended!" [Meaning his uncle.]

The bomb exploded. He sprang towards her with the retort, "Mother, you have *my* father much offended."

She thought that she knew better than he what his dead father had desired.

Then ensued a brief wrangle between these two, mother and son, flesh, bone and soul each of the other,—but a wrangle not unlike, in its pitiable futility, that which often occurs between the sane and the insane person, each helpless to understand and meet the mind of the other.

At last Hamlet stormily commanded,

"Come, come, and sit you down; you shall not budge:
You go not till I set you up a glass
Where you may see the inmost part of you."

Ophelia had seen in his eyes a piteous look as if he had been loosed from hell to speak of horrors.

Gertrude now saw in them a glare as though he had come from hell to execute horrors.

[126]

Then she became that melancholy thing, a mother afraid of her own son, and she cried out,

"What wilt thou do? Thou will not murther me? Help, help, ho!"

Polonius, hearing her, called lustily to summon a guard. Before any one heard and came, Hamlet, thus made aware that some person was listening, exclaimed, "How now! A rat? Dead, for a ducat, dead!" And drawing his rapier, he thrust it through the arras, whence came one gurgling moan, "O, I am slain."

Both the mother and son heard the thud upon the floor of a heavily falling body.

"O me," cried Gertrude, "What hast thou done?"

"Nay, I know not;" said Hamlet, "is it the King?"

Gertrude, knowing that it was not Claudius, hardly noticed this question, and merely lamented, "O what a rash and bloody deed is this!"

Hamlet once more leaped towards her as if he would have choked a confession from her throat.

"A bloody deed!" he muttered between his teeth, "almost as bad, good mother, as kill a king, and marry with his brother."

She answered only, "As kill a king!"

He stared at her and met a bewildered glance. He spoke again, "Ay, lady, 'twas my word."

He stared again. He stared a moment more. Then he yielded to what he saw in her eyes. He saw that she had not suspected that he meant to charge her with having killed the dead King. He saw that she had not suspected that he thought that anybody had killed that King.

She had indeed merely referred the words to his own fancy, that he had himself killed King Claudius, when he drove his sword through the arras. As for "marry with his brother,"—those words, spoken in that connection, had fallen on her astounded ears like meaningless pebbles, reminiscences of the interrupted drama,—more proofs of his lunacy.

Hamlet did not stop to think it out, but in that moment he realized, as a finality, that he could extort no confession from her of complicity in his father's murder, because she had not been a party to it.

He drew the body from behind the curtain into the room, and let it lie at his mother's feet. Perceiving who it was, he vented his usual feelings towards Ophelia's father.

"Thou wretched, rash, intruding fool, farewell,
I took thee for thy better."

Gertrude of Denmark

Being obliged now to relinquish one cause of offense against his mother, he took up his other one, with the stimulated emotion of a fury that has been forced back from its first onset.

This young man who, through a previous hour of this same evening, had been emptying sensual suggestion into the captive mind of a helpless girl, now proceeded to admonish the woman who had borne him, upon the subject of personal holiness.

He bade her stop wringing her hands over the dead body, and "sit down" while he should wring her heart, "for so I shall," he said, "if it be made of penetrable stuff, if damned custom have not braz'd it so that it is proof and bulwark against sense."

She raised her eyes to his, and assuming a tone of maternal authority, she asked,

"What have I done, that thou darest wag thy tongue
In noise so rude against me?"

With impetuous rush came his answer.

"Such an act
That blurs the grace and blush of modesty,
Calls virtue hypocrite, takes off the rose
From the fair forehead of an innocent love

And sets a blister there, makes marriage vows
As false as dicers' oaths; O, such a deed
As from the body of contraction plucks
The very soul, and sweet religion makes
A rhapsody of words; heaven's face doth glow,
Yea, this solidity and compound mass,
With tristful visage, as against the doom,
Is thought-sick at the act."

Her senses sank, drowned in the torrent of his words. All that she really knew, at that moment, was that she did not know, in the least, what he was talking about.

To her apprehension, his speech was a medley of involved sentences expressing unrelated ideas concerning oaths, contracts, hypocrisy, solidity, compound masses and dooms;—words that beat upon her ears, pounded her flesh, and stabbed her like thrusts of his rapier.

As he spoke on, she looked at the corpse lying near, and she saw the blood that stained its clothing. Yet again, she dared to ask him to say plainly what was the act of hers at which thought itself grew sick.

After this, Hamlet began to describe his father with imagery, which stirred within her every quivering memory of love and sorrow. King Hamlet stood before her "mind's eye," as his son pictured him, and her heart was almost stilled in suspended ecstasy at that vision.

A tender scene came suddenly to her recollection. She saw the King holding the boy Hamlet, then about six years old, in his arms. He was putting his hand on the child's head. He said, as she had then thought, very unwisely, "You are a beautiful little prince;" and the child, turned up adoring eyes to his father and replied, "You are the biggest and the handsomest king I ever saw."

Soft tears moistened Gertrude's eyes as she recalled that incident, while her son was saying in his thrilling voice:

"Look here, upon this picture, and on this,
The counterfeit presentment of two brothers.
See, what a grace was seated on this brow:
Hyperion's curls; the front of Jove himself;
An eye like Mars, to threaten and command;
A station like the herald Mercury
New-lighted on the heaven-kissing hill;
A combination and a form indeed,
Where every god did seem to set his seal,
To give the world assurance of a man."

A feeling of triumphant gladness surged through

her. She became so wholly in sympathy with what Hamlet was uttering, that she felt that now once more she and her son were in complete accord, were sharing in a holy sort of communion, partaking together of an exalted memory.

But, in that instant of rapture and of love, all power really passed away from Gertrude to defend herself against that which was yet to fall from Hamlet's lips.

For there did come an after moment, when his speech attained to such a pitch of insolence, that, his mother though she was, being still a woman, she might have had the impulse to strike him dead, had it not been for the effect upon her of that brief period of united feeling,

"This was your husband;"—with these words he ended his apotheosizing rhapsody.

Then came the blast which laid her spirit low, like a withered blossom on the tormented earth, whence foul worms seemed crawling forth to devour all beauty.

Yet, throughout the panegyric pronounced upon the dead King, as well as through the savage diatribe later hurled against Claudius, Gertrude did faintly perceive that one curious element pervaded all that her son said.

Gertrude of Denmark

It was of physical beauty or physical ugliness
of which Hamlet spoke. "Hyperion's curls,"
"the front of Jove," or "a mildew'd ear." . . .
His similes conveyed ideas relevant only to the flesh.

She had been feeding on a mountain, and her son,
her own child, accused her of having left that fair
height "to batten on a moor," and he talked of the
"rebellious hell" that might mutine in a "matron's
bones."

For a few minutes, she struggled not to let her
reason be whirled downward in the cataract of his
speech. To some degree, she realized that Hamlet
had failed wholly to understand that, so far as Claudius had won her affection, he had won it because he
had sought her companionship as an equal. King
Hamlet had treated her mainly as a lovely plaything.
She had indeed been happiest when she was a lovely
plaything; but that was because of some temperamental difference in the men. Claudius could not
have pleased her, as King Hamlet could, by the plaything method. But she had liked to receive the def-
erence due to an equal, which Claudius accorded
to her.

All her effort, not to be wholly overthrown by her
son's abuse, became futile as he continued. Everything he said was dreadful, in itself, apart from any

[133]

question of its justice or its truth,—doubly so, as coming from the lips of a man-child to its mother.

He dealt only in material figures. He denounced her second marriage as unspeakable foulness. He pictured her life as though she sat, not upon a throne but on a heap of garbage. He attributed to her not even the motive of amiable weakness.

Yet he spoke no word which carried the suggestion, that he was charging her with having had a guilty relation with Claudius during his father's lifetime. Neither did he refer to the question whether the marriage were incestuous. Whatever may have been his opinion just then on those matters, he made neither of these accusations. And she gathered no such implication from his words. He merely represented her marriage as impure in itself, because he held it to be impossible that it could be the fruit of any kindly human impulse.

His words were like heavy wheels rolling over her, grinding her down,—and yet, at that very moment, he looked to her like a great angel of wrath. She could not resist him. Can a woman contend with a comet when primal forces shall have loosed it from its moorings?

Or was it terribly, gloriously true that he was an archangel preaching the doctrine of some mighty

righteousness, which she had never apprehended.
Or was he simply a madman?

Then another feeling, rather than thought, came.
And, whatever Hamlet seemed to her at that instant,
this feeling coming upon her and gripping her throat,
stung her into conscious agony.

Had she, after all, been moved to that marriage by
the slightest unworthy desire? Oh God, had she?
Had she in the least, wanted throne and royalty, for
herself, and not merely for Hamlet? This thought
hissed its awful question in her ears.

It hissed, because, of course, in a sense it was true
that she had been partly influenced to marry Claudius
because she wanted something for herself. She had
preferred life to stagnation and, constituted and situ-
ated as she was, such a marriage had meant life and
opportunity,—while retreat to a convent had meant
dreariness and stagnation.

There were, indeed, women, even in her period,
who, as spinsters or widows, could, and did carve out
and carry on interesting and useful careers for themselves in politics or other action.

Gertrude was not that kind, and nothing, in her
experience as King Hamlet's wife, had fitted her to become such. For her the choice was, as I have stated
it, either stagnation in a convent or perhaps as a

mere idle appendage in the Court,—or else the continuance of gracious and socially beneficent existence as a wife and queen.

She had made the normal choice. But, at this moment, with her son standing before her and hurling accusing epithets at her, it seemed that every motive which had influenced her must have been stained through by some terrible stream of selfishness, flowing outward from her soul, as the blood of an old man was even then soaking out from flesh through garments to the rug upon the floor at her feet.

And now returned her earlier moral question. Was the marriage really one that was forbidden by God's law? And, if it were, had she herself become an odious creature?

Then it was that she sobbed,

"O Hamlet, speak no more;
Thou turn'st mine eyes into my very soul,
And there I see such black and grained spots
As will not leave their tint."

Out of her very innocence, as many another stormily distracted one has done, she confessed to a comparatively small fault, in language which sounded like the admission of a great sin.

[136]

Gertrude of Denmark

Her momentarily sincere, but over emphasized, humility availed her nothing in its impact with the hard, unsympathetic passion of Hamlet's self-centred nature.

He went on, "Nay, but to live stewed in corruption."

This ground out from her a deeper groan,

"O, speak to me no more;
These words like daggers enter in mine ears;
No more, sweet Hamlet."

Neither her groan, nor her loving word stopped him.

Hamlet now turned his speech against the character and not merely the person of Claudius.

"A murtherer and a villain," he cried, but this phrase did not arouse in his mother the suspicion which he expected it to produce. Gertrude took it only in a general sense. It was a common thing in that age for one man to kill another with his own hand or by proxy; and Gertrude had often heard a man applauded by his friends for taking another's life and condemned by his enemies, as a murderer, for the same deed; or she had heard him lightly accused by foes of something he had never done.

Distracted by his own knowledge of his uncle's

guilt, Hamlet did not duly steer the course of his language to its destined port. In a moment more, he came to feel that it would be unwise to let his mother see that he suspected that his father had been murdered.

He hastily turned the subject and his next words struck upon her consciousness to plainer effect. He called Claudius

"A cutpurse of the empire and the rule,
That from a shelf the precious diadem stole,
And put it in his pocket."

When he said that, Gertrude felt a sudden sense of relief. She thought that he referred to the fact that Claudius, rather than himself, had received the election to the throne, and that he was uttering a vague accusation that the election had been procured by unfair pressure upon the electorate. She knew nothing about this matter, and her innate loyalty led her to brush the charge aside as a mere annoyance.

She said again, "No more."

Hamlet heeded her as little as she had heeded this last count in the catalogue of his objections to her husband. He went on, "A king of shreds and patches."—

Then, apparent only to Hamlet, came the great

Ghost, whom she could not see; and everything she had been feeling, every bit of pain and agony was swept clean out of her, by a gust of wonder, as she saw her son suddenly pause and stare into what was vacancy to her senses.

Silent amazement held them both for some seconds till, in low musical tones, he began addressing that which seemed to her like empty space.

"Save me and hover o'er me with your wings,
    You heavenly guards!—What would your gracious
        figure?"

Voice and shape, all was beautiful, but his mother's heart yearned towards that beauty of his with infinite pity.

"Alas," she whispered, "he's mad!"

Nothing else mattered to her now. She forgot that he had reproached her; she forgot that he had insulted her; she forgot all about Claudius; she forgot her lately aroused love for the dead King . . . nothing now mattered on earth, nor, so far as she was concerned, in heaven itself:—nothing but her boy, her creation, her Hamlet!

She did not hear the voice of the Ghost which Hamlet heard replying to his adjurations. She did not hear it even when Hamlet heard it bid him be more gentle with his mother. But when after what seemed to her a long silence in the room, her son turned and said lovingly, "How is it with you, lady?" she burst into tender tears.

She gazed at him through this mist of mournful love. She saw his face lighted by unearthly radiance,—yet, knowing not what he had seen and heard, that radiance to her seemed born of disaster.

Figures of tragedy, they stood thus,—neither comprehending the other,—each being infused throughout by a supreme passion.

Then she opened her heart of motherhood and spilled its holy contents at his feet. She reached her hand out to touch him and drew it back in fear. But she had begun to speak and her voice flowed on as though it had been that of Hecuba herself.

"Alas, how is't with you,
That you do bend your eye on vacancy
And with the incorporal air do hold discourse;—
Forth at your eyes, your spirits wildly peep;
And as the sleeping soldiers in the alarm,
Your bedded hair, like life in excrements
Starts up, and stands an end. O gentle son,
Upon the heat and flame of thy distemper
Sprinkle cool patience. Whereon do you look?"

Gertrude of Denmark

"On him, on him," he cried earnestly.

        "Look you, how pale he glares!
His form and cause conjoin'd, preaching to stones,
Would make them capable—"

He turned and moved somewhat away from her,
and continued, as speaking to another,

        "Do not look upon me;
Lest with this piteous action you convert
My stern effects: then what I have to do
Will want true colour; tears perchance for blood."

Love made her bold to try to follow this changing
spirit of her son into mystery. She asked, "To
whom do you speak thus?"

He answered question with question, "Do you see
nothing there?"

She was brave to make true reply even to a madman, "Nothing at all; yet all that is, I see."

"Nor did you nothing hear?" he persisted.

"No, nothing but ourselves."

He caught her hand and turned her into the attitude of direct vision.

"Why, look you there!" he half commanded, half
entreated, "look how it steals away!"

He said "it" not "he," as though he were doubtful

what it was that his eyes did perceive. Then he braced himself, and spoke resolutely,

"My father, in his habit as he liv'd!
Look, where he goes, even now, out at the portal!"

She answered gently,

"This is the very coinage of your brain;
This bodiless creation ecstasy
Is very cunning in."

She sank down on a couch during the argument which he proceeded to make to prove his sanity. It was not medically a very sound argument. But she did not know that. She was wishing he would lie at her feet and put his head on her knees, as he had so lately done with Ophelia. She was wishing that, even while he was talking about her "trespass" and speaking of "weeds" and "compost." She scarcely noted his words at this time.

She had resolved that she would not again contradict anything he said. She had heard it was not wise to dispute with persons who were crazed.

At last, he paused so long that she felt obliged to say something. Out of her infinite sorrow on his account, she spoke the simple truth,

"O Hamlet, thou hast cleft my heart in twain."

Gertrude of Denmark

He took this for a confession of sin in that heart of hers—welcomed it as such. He said rather tenderly,

> "O, throw away the worser part of it,
> And live the purer with the other half.
> Good night."

She neither understood nor cared for his words. She felt a great yet most mournful joy in the tenderness of his voice.

But he went on to admonish her again with savage brutality in relation to her marriage. She shut her lips tight and did not answer, and would not have answered, had the consequence of her silence been Hamlet's throttling hand around her neck. What mother would discuss her own marriage relation with her son, were he sane or insane?

She did not now even command him to be still. She had nothing now to say about his rude and noisy tongue. The awful doom of his madness had made him immune from her reproach. Silence—tender silence . . . with that as with a mantle to cover his ruin, she confronted him—her child.

After his harangue had ended with "one word more, good lady," she asked quietly, "What shall I do?"

He bade her promise not to tell Claudius that he "essentially" was "not in madness." She gave the promise, willingly enough, since such omission of speech was quite in accord with her conviction that he was essentially "in madness."

They had a little converse together about his going to England. He talked, as she thought, very wildly about delving into mines, blowing things to the moon and other inappropriate and senseless themes.

Finally, however, he did bend over the dead body of Polonius, and to her deep satisfaction, he did speak one reverent word. She also saw, or made herself think that she saw, tears in his eyes, and she would not let herself recognize the mockery in his tone as he addressed the corpse of Ophelia's father, "Come, sir, to draw towards an end with you."

When in a yearning, almost childlike tone, Hamlet, for the fifth time, said "Good night, mother," Gertrude's heart melted. She started towards him as towards her baby—then stopped motionless, as before mystery,—and let him go untouched by her.

She slowly placed herself on a couch near the door into her sleeping room. As she did so, she remembered a morning hour, seven and twenty years before, when she came alone through that door and

[144]

found, lying there, the child Hamlet, a little figure that seemed to be all curls and white garments around and below a small pale face.

He was feeling slightly sick, and he had escaped from attendants and come by himself to lie close to the threshold of her room. There, without a cry, he lay patiently waiting for her to come, bend over and lift him up.

She stayed beside him all that day, singing, telling him stories, listening to his chatter, feeding him, soothing him, kissing him awake, watching him sleep. . . . In the glad sunlight then,—where just now he had stood reviling her.

CHAPTER XI

GERTRUDE sat motionless, in the midnight solitude after Hamlet had left, dragging with him the body of Polonius. There was a pool of blood on the floor where it had lain. There were smears of blood on the track along which it had been drawn. They ceased abruptly near the portal, for there Hamlet had stopped and, seizing a piece of tapestry, had wrapped it carefully around the corpse in its bloodstained raiment.

The lights were burning low in the room. Gertrude looked from one crimson spot to another.

After a while, she rose heavily to her feet, staggered a second, recovered her balance, and went alone to one of the King's offices. She found her husband closeted with Rosencrantz and Guildenstern. He looked at her inquiringly.

"I pray you, my lord," she implored, "that you give me leave to rest a moment. I am faint."

She sank on some cushions and, for a few minutes, the silence in the room was broken only by her sobbing breath. The King came and bent over her, saying,

"There's matter in these sighs; these profound heaves
  You must translate; 'tis fit we understand them.
  Where is your son?"

She sent the young men out and then began to cry harder than before. The King laid his hand on her shoulder. She made one or two efforts to tell her story, and he asked "How does Hamlet?"
Then she succeeded in sobbing a reply.

"Mad as the sea and wind, when both contend
  Which is the mightier; in his lawless fit,
  Behind the arras hearing something stir,
  Whips out his rapier, cries, 'A rat, a rat!'
  And in this brainish apprehension kills
  The unseen good old man."

Claudius made an answer, in which expressions of genuine feeling were marvellously well stitched together with utterances of the most damnable hypocrisy.

It is probable that, at this moment, while he was talking, Claudius began to plan to have Hamlet put to death in England; having at first intended merely to get him away from Denmark.

Gertrude of Denmark

The mock play had made Claudius realize that Hamlet suspected him of having murdered the late King. He had since appealed to Heaven for pardon and protection. He had come to feel that Heaven would not forgive and shield him; and now that stab through the arras had taught him that Hamlet's sword might strike him unawares at any minute. Heaven and Earth were thus leagued against him. He must save himself, though to do so were to dare Hell to join the forces with which he was contending.

Of course, Gertrude did not recognize the hypocrisy in this speech of Claudius', nor did she perceive the terrible undertow to its outward meaning, but she did see the truth of his assertion that had he, himself, been there, he and not Polonius, would have been killed.

She could not fail to find it evident that Hamlet's freaks were endangering any or everybody with whom he came in contact, but she made her tender plea in his behalf, when asked where he had gone.

"To draw apart the body he hath kill'd;
O'er whom his very madness, like some ore
Among a mineral of metals base,
Shows itself pure. He weeps for what is done."

She could not object to the King's proposal to start

Hamlet that very morning on the embassy to England, and to use all their "majesty and skill" to both "countenance and excuse" the murder of Polonius.

Rosencrantz and Guildenstern returned. The King gave them directions to seek out Hamlet, "speak him fair, and bring the body into the chapel."

All this sounded well to Gertrude, as well as anything could in the horrible situation, but when, as she and Claudius were finally leaving the room, he said, "O come away! My soul is full of discord and dismay;" something within her protested against his egoism.

She thought of her own soul and the sorrow that filled it. She thought of Ophelia's young soul, and the dismay that would brim its crystal goblet when she should learn her father's fate. She rebuked her own soul, however, and assured it that Claudius was infinitely kind in all plans and purposes.

An hour later, having, during the interim, been employed in his more private office, Claudius had Hamlet brought to him. He saw the Prince in the presence of Rosencrantz and Guildenstern, and formally announced to him that he was to start immediately on the mission to England. After this everybody left the King in the chamber where he stayed alone for a little while pondering on the whole aspect of affairs.

The Great Wizard, following the necessary theatrical custom of rendering the thoughts of a person by spoken soliloquies, thus gives to the world and all the ages, the substance of the King's thoughts,

> "England, if my love thou hold'st at aught—
> . . . thou may'st not coldly set
> Our sovereign process; which imports at full,
> By letters conjuring to that effect,
> The present death of Hamlet.   Do it, England;
> For like the hectic in my blood he rages,
> And thou must cure me: till I know 'tis done,
> Howe'er my haps, my joys were ne'er begun."

In this decision to ask England to put Hamlet to death, the one great intellectual weakness of Claudius showed itself.   In any critical hour which was to him an hour of extreme terror lest retributive evil should befall him, he almost invariably planned a mistaken way of escape, one certain to lead to more disaster.

So now terror was driving him to adopt a most dangerous expedient, such as only frenzy could have suggested, for if England should obey his behest, formal and definite report thereof was likely to be made by the English authorities to Denmark.   Such report could hardly be kept secret from many persons. Gertrude might hear of it.

The probability of such final event is manifested by the fact that in Shakspeare's story, quite public proclamation is made of the action taken in the matter.

In relation to his marriage, Claudius had also blundered. He married Gertrude because he loved her beautiful presence and her gentle nature, but he married hastily in the mistaken conviction that the sooner he did it the more certainly would the union strengthen his position as king. The opposite thing happened. That hurry stirred Hamlet to hatred and aroused his vague suspicion.

The delay of a few months might have softened the shock of the marriage to Hamlet, when it did occur, and might therefore have changed the whole course of events.

As things were, Hamlet often doubted the Ghost. Had he not been moved to anger by haste he might have disregarded the Ghost's admonitions to the extent of continued inaction.

And, but for that speedy arrangement for a wedding festivity to follow so hard upon the funeral pageant, is it not (shall I say) spiritually possible, that the Ghost Himself, or Itself, although aware of the fact of the poisoning, might not have come to suspect adultery or to accuse the mother to the son?

This last suggestion is, I admit, a speculation anent supernatural mysteries, and is here offered with proper humility by the present chronicler. I do, nevertheless, make bold to express surprise that most critics should have refrained for centuries from studying the character and the intellect of Claudius, the murderer of his brother, and the husband of Gertrude, erstwhile Dowager of Denmark.

There have been a few writers who have shown some discernment when treating of Claudius. Mainly however, he has been written of or ignored as though he possessed no idiosyncrasies whatever, and as if he might be pictorially represented on canvas by one shapeless, shadeless smirch of complete blackness.

Ophelia had gone to her father's house immediately after the queen had seen her in the corridor, at the close of the play.

She was kneeling in her closet, and the early morning light was streaming in through a narrow window. A hand was pressed against each temple, her eyes were closed, her body held rigidly still, when a servant entered and told her that her father had been stabbed to death.

The woman added a pious falsehood, which may indeed have been merely the repetition of a rumor which the King himself had thought best to start on its rounds. It was to the effect, that Polonius had not died till after a priest had come and had administered the last rites. "He made a good end," said the servant.

"Who stabbed him?" asked Ophelia.

"It must not be mentioned," stammered the servant, "but 'tis said that the Prince mistook him for some ruffian hidden in the queen's room."

The servant heard Ophelia make a low moaning utterance before she fainted quite away. Her words were, "The Prince did say my father played the fool."

After that, Ophelia was never known to mention Hamlet directly. All report, however, of her later speech and song, makes it evident that a shadowy, only half recognized image kept appearing and disappearing amid her other fancies,—the image of a lover who had injured her soul.

Her straying memory, her weakened faculties, permitted her to reveal her consciousness of that haunting presence, only in the language of such songs of offered girlish love and its betrayal, as she had heard sung by shepherdesses in the pastures around the little river, whose banks had been forbidden to the footsteps of a queen, but where she had strolled in innocent freedom.

So far as his mother knew, Hamlet said and did nothing during his last hours, before he left Denmark, which would indicate that he had any thought of the girl whose father he had killed. But she did hear from various sources, of his flippant speeches about the dead man and the supper which the worms were to have of his body. "Madness, mere madness," she said to the King. "Alas, how his malady has deformed him."

She did not herself see her son again before his departure; nor did she receive any message from him.

CHAPTER XII

THE night after Hamlet left Elsinore, his mother slept from sheer exhaustion, and for the first time in the forty-eight hours which were marked by its conclusion. She had a troubled dream of King Hamlet from which she awoke trembling. She slept again in helpless weakness; the dream returned, and again she awoke in throbbing terror.

She continued for many succeeding nights to have these disturbing dreams. They all had one general purport. She was young in them, and the King had gone from her, as indeed, in his life time, he had often gone and stayed away for months together, on expeditions of regal piracy, of regal robbery and regal slaughter. True to the education she had received, Gertrude had always supposed his expeditions to be in quest of glory and grandeur or even for the performance of duty.

In these dreams there was something terrible and mysterious about her husband's absences. She did not know when he had left her or whither he had gone. No tidings of him came back to her. She seemed to be moving through an atmosphere, which was like a black cloud around her,—a cloud outside and yet somehow a part of herself, or rather part of her inner agony. She tried to cry and could not make a sound, to ask, she knew not whom, why no messenger came from the King to her.

In this mock enactment of life, she went sobbing from stone-walled turret to turret, and always she carried the baby Hamlet on her breast.

Often she came to some place whence retreat was suddenly closed, and where, would she go forward, as go she must, she would have to leap across deep trenches grooved between castles.

Everything, everywhere at which she looked was either stone or blackened space. Everything was misty and meaningless or else was hard to her touch —hard like stone,—everything save the soft little body in her arms.

Once the scene was much changed. Stony ledges took the place of the castle walls, which usually hemmed in her unreal march, and she was struggling to walk through thickets, or underbrush, in the quarries. She had some thought in her mind which was only distantly related to anything that had ever happened to her on the solid earth. She saw a dark shape in the distance, and she discovered that she could make a vocal sound. She cried to the phantasmagoric figure,

"O, I'd marry King Hamlet,—if he would only come back to me."

Then she became again conscious of the baby whose head was upon her shoulder, and she sobbed, "Why I am married to him already,"—and so sobbing, she awoke, . . . and heard the deep breathing of Claudius at her side.

Immediately after the death of her father, Ophelia and her aunt, with a maid, had been assigned an apartment in the castle. There the girl became very ill and was shut in closely by her guardians, while the house, in which she and Laertes had lived with their father, was occupied only by servants. Gertrude had insisted on this arrangement, not thinking it well for the orphan to stay in her former home before her brother should return.

The Queen shrank from seeing Ophelia, lest the girl should ask questions which it would not be well to answer. But soon a stupor came over the child, and when Gertrude then entered the room, no word was spoken by either of them. Gertrude came out from the chamber panic stricken.

That night she dreamed of kneeling in the court-

yard of the castle and beseeching King Hamlet not
to go on some projected journey.

"It will be cold and lonesome," she cried.
"There is snow on the valleys; there is ice on
the little river under the willows, and the baby is
sick."

The dream king kissed . . . and vanished.

Gertrude became aware that disquieting rumors
were afloat. People had grown suspicious that
something was rotten in Denmark. The hurried and
rather secret burial of Polonius, the departure of the
foremost Prince of the realm, the stories of his
bizarre speech and senseless actions, during the preceding months, these things were developing a gos-
siping and restless spirit in the multitude. People
suspected that evil was abroad in the land; yet no
evidence appeared to indicate that anybody had got
hold of the idea that Claudius had murdered the
late King. No whisper to that effect buzzed around
in the Danish world.

In all the daytime of this period, however else
she was outwardly occupied, Gertrude was thinking
of her son. The thought of Ophelia was like a
shadow thrown across her mind from that thought of

him. But she never failed to be gentle and sympathetic with Claudius; she never doubted him at all, and her affection for him retained its lifelong quality of calm solidity.

CHAPTER XIII

AFTER two or three weeks had passed, Ophelia's malady suddenly became that of garrulous insanity. She escaped from her rooms and roved about the castle and out into the adjoining country. As she went she babbled and sang. Some mysterious beauty in her personality, some spiritually pathetic effluence seemed blown outward from her like a soft wind. Its fragrance subdued her attendants so that they let her wander where she would. "God is leading her," they said and crossed themselves.

She did not remember many persons, nor did she always appear to recognize, when in their presence, the very ones of whom she had spoken with a sort of recollection. But she always kept some persistent memory of the woman who had led her to the meeting which, she had been persuaded, would be the occasion for her betrothal. So she roamed about calling for the Queen; and at last, Horatio and one of the gentlemen-in-waiting took it upon themselves to acquaint Gertrude with the situation,

Gertrude of Denmark

Ophelia being then held at bay just outside the royal apartments.

"I will not speak with her," said Gertrude. To face another encounter with a lunatic was horrible to this woman who, except for that frightful hour with Hamlet, had throughout all her adult life been cloistered in splendor and sheathed in courtesy. Moreover, she did not then know, as she later learned from the servant's confession, that Ophelia had been told whose rapier it was that had let out her father's life. She still feared, as she had from the beginning, that, if she saw the daughter, she would in some way reveal the awful secret of that stab through the arras. This fear, and the knowledge from which it grew, wrought an uneasiness like that of guilt within her. Her objection yielded at last to the representations made to her, by Horatio and his companion, that her continued refusal to see the girl might arouse "dangerous conjectures in ill-breeding minds."

"Let her come in," she said, and then waited sick with apprehension, while Horatio went out and brought Ophelia back with him.

The girl glanced wistfully around, without seeming to see, and moaned a question, "Where is the beauteous Majesty of Denmark?"

Gertrude's fear passed. She felt only pity and love. She moved forward, saying, "How now, Ophelia?"

The girl shrank away, apparently not timidly, but in a daze of other feeling. She began to sing,

> "How should I your true love know
> From another one?
> By his cockle hat and staff,
> And his sandal shoon."

To this wild warble, which bore no suggestion relevant to Gertrude's inner thought, she asked tenderly, "Alas, sweet lady, what imports this song?"

But the words of the next stanza went quivering yet straight to the hurt spot in the Queen's foreboding heart.

> "He is dead and gone, lady,
> He is dead and gone;
> At his head a grass-green turf,
> At his heels a stone."

"Nay, but, Ophelia,"—Gertrude began in an expostulating tone, but paused, and the woeful singing continued,

> "White his shroud as the mountain snow—"

Gertrude of Denmark

The entrance of Claudius interrupted the rendition of this ballad, and while Ophelia was silent, Gertrude went swiftly to the King with the instinctive movement of a trustful wife.

"Alas, look here, my lord," she whispered.

And let everyone take note,—Claudius was gentle to Ophelia, who resumed her singing,

> "Larded with sweet flowers;
> Which bewept to the grave did go
> With true-love showers."

"How do you, pretty lady?" asked the King.

She responded with a low bow and a wavering gesture of her white hand,—the whole movement somehow more bird-like than human,—yet indescribably tender and childlike also.

Thus swaying, she said, "Well, God 'ield you," then remembering the old legend of what befell the girl who had refused charity to the Saviour, she smiled just a little and added, "They say the owl was a baker's daughter."

She threw her glance upward, looked like a statue of prayer, and murmured, "Lord, we know what we are, but know not what we may be," then said in a louder tone, "God be at your table," and ending thus, she seemed to dissolve from the statue she had been into a bending spirit of reverent courtesy, gracefully saluting both their Majesties.

"Conceit upon her father," said the King, essaying interpretation. Did Ophelia half understand? She straightened herself, and looked as though she were struggling to think out something clearly and to say it. She contracted her brows, her eyes grew misty, then she attempted her answer.

"Pray you, let's have no words of this, but when they ask you what it means, say you this"—she broke off and was silent, while Gertrude held her breath in dismayed wonder what Ophelia would say that it did mean.

Suddenly the girl smiled again, but the smile was sadder than it had been before. Her lips parted and she sang—the old, old song that has rung through all the ages and in all the climes of this earth,—the song of love and its betrayal.

"Pretty Ophelia!" said the King in a soft, low whisper, as the singing flowed on like a rippling brook to the whirlpool.

Gertrude felt that the very air of the room was flooded with pain when, at last, Ophelia swept another courtesy, and once more tried to speak plain sentences. Her words fluttered up and down and over the trembling thought that lay submerged in her mind, as a swallow dips itself and starts upward again from the waters which it just touches now and then.

"I hope all will be well. We must be patient; but I cannot choose but weep, to think they should lay him i' the cold ground. My brother shall know of it; and so I thank you for your good counsel.—Come, my coach!—Good night, ladies; good night, sweet ladies; good night, good night."

Having spoken thus, she passed from the interview that she had sought with such insistence, but through which she had appeared to drift without purpose. Had her speech fallen like barren sand on the desert of time?

So soon as Ophelia had vanished from his pitying sight, the King sent Horatio to see that she was properly cared for. Then he turned to his queen;

"O Gertrude, Gertrude," he said, "when sorrows come, they come not single spies, but in battalions."

He enumerated his troubles; the death of Polonius, the departure of Hamlet after much perplexing conduct; and he said he had come to feel that it had been a mistake to bury the body of Polonius so hastily and with such scant ceremony. It had "mud-

[165]

died" the minds of the people and stirred them up
to discontented question. Worst of all he added,
Ophelia's brother

> "is in secret come from France,
> Feeds on his wonder, keeps himself in clouds,
> And wants not buzzers to infect his ear
> With pestilent speeches of his father's death;
> Wherein necessity, of matter beggar'd,
> Will nothing stick our person to arraign
> In ear and ear.   O my dear Gertrude, this,
> Like to a murthering-piece, in many places
> Gives me superfluous death."

She listened aghast at all the possibilities of disaster thus outlined; and even as the King spoke, the
uproar of outside tumult broke in upon their senses.
Gertrude had never before heard such an ominous
sound.   "Alack," she cried, "What noise is that?"

"Where are my Switzers?" demanded Claudius,
going towards the entrance, "Let them guard the
door."

An attendant rushed in exclaiming, "Save yourself, my lord."

Claudius caught Gertrude's hand as she stepped to
his side, and both stood facing the man while he
continued,

Gertrude of Denmark

> "Laertes, in a riotous head,
> O'erbears your officers. The rabble call him lord;
> They cry, 'Choose we; Laertes shall be king!'
> Caps, hands, and tongues applaud it to the clouds,
> 'Laertes shall be king, Laertes king!'"

Gertrude threw back her head and said scornfully, "How cheerfully on the false trail they cry! O, this is counter, you false Danish dogs!"

In a moment more, they all heard the crash of broken doors; and Laertes came in fully armed. A crowd of excited men followed him. He turned them back, and after a moment's protest, they obeyed and retreated into the corridor.

Laertes threw a glance, a gesture and a word towards the mob as it retired, "I thank you; keep the door." Then he walked straight up before his sovereigns and hurled his speech directly at their faces.

> "O thou vile king, give me my father!"

Gertrude let go of the King's hand, went close to the young man and took hold of his. She had often held him on her knee when he was a child. Custom paralyzed him. He stood still.

"Calmly, good Laertes," she said with a smile,

that was only a little more dauntless than it was gracious.

He did not withdraw from her, but still facing Claudius, he proceeded,

"That drop of blood that's calm, proclaims me bas-
tard,
Cries cuckold to my father, brands the harlot
Even here, between the chaste unsmirched brows
Of my true mother."

The King in his answer spoke considerately, as though he realized that Laertes' fury was natural, and he manifested no timidity. Claudius was cow-ardly, only before his own conscience and his pow-erful imagination of possible retribution. He asked quietly,

"What is the cause, Laertes,
That thy rebellion looks so giantlike?"

Then turning to the Queen, he continued,

"Let him go, Gertrude; do not fear our person:
There's such divinity doth hedge a king,
That treason can but peep to what it would,
Acts little of his will.—Tell me, Laertes,

[168]

Gertrude of Denmark

Why thou art thus incens'd.—Let him go, Gertrude,—
Speak, man."

Gertrude admired her husband just then. She lifted her hand and let it fall slowly to her side. She half smiled at Claudius and moved backward a little from both the men.

"Where is my father?" demanded Laertes.

"Dead," answered the King.

"But not by him," said the Queen pointing to Claudius.

She spoke no other word, and the King talked with Laertes aside, so that she did not quite fully hear what was said.

Then came new outcry in the corridor, the followers of Laertes clustered there were heard insisting that someone should be let to come into the hall.

Ophelia entered, babbling, singing and bringing flowers. She gave no certain sign that she recognized her brother, even while he lamented over her. She merely stood still and sang;

> "They bore him barefac'd on the bier;
> Hey non nonny, nonny, hey nonny;
> And on his grave rains many a tear.—
> Fare you well, my dove!"

[169]

Gertrude of Denmark

The eyes of Laertes were too full of dismay to permit the flow of tears when Ophelia began to distribute her flowers. She gave him rosemary and pansies.

She handed sprigs of fennel and of columbine to the King, and she stood motionless a moment before going slowly to the Queen who was now sitting on a chair. She knelt and laid her head against the knee of the woman who had once led her to meet Hamlet. Gertrude smoothed the tumbled hair on that tired little head. Ophelia drew herself away far enough to gaze into the other's face, and handing her some sprays, murmured, "There's rue for you."

Then she plucked with fickle movement among the blossoms that remained in her basket, found some more rue, and put it in her own bosom,—smiled piteously up into the Queen's tender eyes, and said, "here's some for me; we may call it herb of grace o' Sundays."

She laid her head down again, lifted it, and said very softly, "Oh, you must wear your rue with a difference."

She put a starry blossom into a fold of Gertrude's gown, and babbled on: "There's a daisy: I would give you some violets, but they withered all when my father died; they say he made a good end."

Gertrude of Denmark

The wild, pitiful warbling began once more, and, disengaging herself, from the Queen's arms, which had been enfolding her, the girl arose and wandered unsteadily here and there, singing,

"For bonny sweet Robin is all my joy."

Then, pausing momentarily before one and the other of her silent listeners she sang,

"And will he not come again?
And will he not come again?
　　No, no, he is dead;
　　Go to thy death bed,
He never will come again.
His beard was white as snow,
All flaxen was his poll;
　　He is gone, he is gone,
　　And we cast away moan:
God ha' mercy on his soul."

Waving her hand in a salute which included them all, she added, "And of all Christian souls, I pray God.—God be wi' ye."

She drifted away as on the wind of her own ecstasy, went out through the portal, and the crowd in the corridor parted to let her pass.

Gertrude of Denmark

The King talked on quietly to Laertes, promising to satisfy him as to his own innocence in the matter of his father's death. Gertrude half hid herself in an alcove beside a great stone fireplace. The King and Laertes softly left the room together. Gertrude went alone until she met her maids at another doorway.

CHAPTER XIV

GERTRUDE pondered compassionately on Ophelia's words and finished by pitying both herself and the girl.

"She is daft," said the Queen to her own heart, "Yet the maid still knows that she and I are both stricken creatures. She wears rue because of her father's death, and because of the mad Prince who has gone to England. I wear rue for the Prince's sake and for that of his dead father. But I can wear mine openly for the Prince, and not for his father. She, poor wench, may wear hers openly for her father, but not for the Prince who did not wed her."

Gertrude did not know that Laertes had once bidden his sister to think of Hamlet's love as "a violet in the youth of primy nature." Therefore Ophelia's words, "I would give you violets but they withered all when my father died," aroused in the Queen no mournful wonder, whether they were prompted by any associated thought of a lost love and a broken hope.

It does not matter though whether Ophelia's bab-
blings were infused by that memory. All the violets
of life had withered for the girl during those twenty-
four hours, in the course of which, Hamlet had cast
her from him, had insulted her maidenhood and
killed her father.

Claudius and Laertes were closeted together for
an hour that day, but their conference was interrupted by the coming of some nobles on business
which would not permit of delay, and Laertes was
persuaded to hold himself and his followers in check
until the morrow when he was to see the King again.

That night, Gertrude dreamed that she was walking in a rocky ice-covered field, carrying the child
who grew momentarily heavier and heavier. She
kept calling, "My lord; my lord, King Hamlet!"

A blank came in her dream, and then she found
herself sitting down amid stones and ice, under a
midnight sky. She saw the figure of Claudius approaching her.

"Where is the King?" she asked.

"Dead," answered the misty shape which was up-
lifted, like a mirage, in her sleep engendered fancy,
"Dead, but not by me!"

Gertrude of Denmark

She awoke with a cry.

Yet, before this night, all the troubled question, which Hamlet had revived in her mind, as to whether the marriage with Claudius were wrong in itself, had, in some unaccountable fashion, passed quietly away from her. It had gone, without argument or even further thought on her part, like a miasmatic fog silently dispelled by the breeze and the sunshine of morning.

She did, however, continue to be afraid that she had been partly influenced to marry Claudius because she wanted to remain "the beauteous Majesty of Denmark." This fear made her more tender in her treatment of him and more solicitous than ever to attend to all his minor wants.

Early on this morrow, Claudius held a long session with Laertes, whom he convinced that he was entirely free from complicity in the death of Polonius. He said that Hamlet had slain the old man by mistake, probably not even knowing that it was Polonius who was behind the arras when he stabbed, but he told the son of the Prince's many contemptuous speeches about his father, till Laertes was as indignantly moved to resentment, as he might have been by the most intentional murder. Claudius added the statement that Hamlet had pursued his own life.

Laertes asked the King why he had not openly called Hamlet to account.

Claudius waited a moment, before replying, but, when he did speak, he told the truth of himself and of Gertrude. He said he had refrained from accusing Hamlet for two reasons.

One was that the Danish people loved the Prince and might have turned angrily against himself had he denounced Hamlet publicly. The other was (and there was something appealing in the way he made confession thus):

> "The queen, his mother,
> Lives almost by his looks; and for myself—
> My virtue or my plague, be it either which—
> She's so conjunctive to my life and soul,
> That, as the star moves not but in his sphere,
> I could not but by her."

I repeat, Claudius was then speaking a certain truth of himself. His love for Gertrude, though it was a selfish, unmoral love of feeling joy, still was not grossly sensual, and had not been that, from the beginning. With whatever soul he possessed, he had always loved her presence in somewhat the same way that persons, who are not exactly religious, often prefer church to dance music and good music to that which is poor.

He loved her beauty as other men love pictures, and even as other men love nature itself.

He loved her voice as he might have loved, perhaps did love, the rippling sound of sweet waters, or the song of birds above a flowing brook.

If the soul of man, and not merely his senses, be capable of loving the inanimate blossoms of earth or the unattainable clouds of sunset, then Claudius had a soul, and it did love Gertrude, as something "conjunctive" to it.

That quality, in himself and in his love, had made it possible for him to watch her from afar, and make no evil attempt to possess her during thirty years.

But at the last, what was it which sunk that soul of his in the slime of criminality? Was it hatred of some one else, or hatred of some condition then existing in his daily life?

Or, was it that over development of aestheticism, which rots downward into the heart of man, and turns the love of anything, which is beautiful, and of any person who is lovely, into self love and the desire for self gratification?

Laertes felt, momentarily, a little aghast as he listened to the King's revelation, but he was too much preoccupied with his own affairs to give it long consideration.

Just at that instant, Claudius had no plan of revengeful action to unfold to Laertes. He supposed that Hamlet was either still on his way to England, or was there, or had even been already put to death; and he was merely bent on making a friend of the young man. The entrance of a messenger with letters from Hamlet changed the whole situation. Horatio had received one an hour earlier in the day, but the King did not know that fact. They had been brought to the castle by some sailors, who had been on the ship in which Hamlet had now returned to Denmark.

There was a letter to the King and also one to the Queen, but Claudius never gave that to her.

He read his own, and his fertile brain at once conceived an evil scheme. He revealed it instantly to Laertes, who was still excited by all that had been told him of Hamlet's speech about greedy worms and the fleshly corruption of the body, whence he had derived his own passionate young life. He accepted the King's suggestion to assume a friendly attitude towards Hamlet, when he should arrive at Elsinore, to challenge him to an amicable duel of fencing, to use a poisoned rapier and so, by a mere prick which would seem wholly innocent, to kill him.

Poisoning was then a very gentlemanly method by which high-born folk might commit murder. To use such material as poison, in the compassing of his revenge, really raised young Laertes in social rank and set him among the gentry of earth.

While this evil conference was going on, Gertrude learned that Ophelia had been drowned in the willow bordered stream near the castle. A lame peasant woman had watched the scene from afar, had not at first perceived the import of that which she saw, and, when at last she had guessed what was happening, had been unable to reach the spot in time to give either speedy assistance herself or to summon other help.

Shepherd girls and a single country lad, together, finally brought the drenched body into one of the castle gardens. It chanced that the Queen and a few of her waiting ladies were there, and they heard the volubly told story and saw the piteous sight. Gertrude took a dripping wreath of flowers from the cold white fingers.

She knew those flowers. She had often received them from Ophelia's living hand. She had now an immediate vision of blossoms, and she seemed to hear singing and to see blossoms in their season. Blossoms, blossoms, everywhere . . . and a singing voice. Gertrude saw them all, and heard each song.

Suddenly all the poetry in Gertrude's nature awoke, like a spirit, arising from the sunken depths of unconscious being. It was a strange psychical experience,—but it came to her, this woman of primal instincts. She had lived among conventions, she had thought the thoughts which courtiers, princes and abbesses had taught her to think. She had not possessed the intellect, which would have enabled her to unthink them. Love and dignity had sufficed to quiet all impulse towards self-expression. But the stone, which had covered the sanctuary of her inner life, was now rolled away. Tragedy touched and transformed her into one who must sing aloud.

The need for utterance became greater, for the moment, even than her grief or her horror because of Ophelia's death. Memories of hours passed with the girl over baskets of blossoms, and the talk of the shepherd women supplied her with imagery. She rushed into the presence of Claudius and Laertes, not so much like a stricken mourner, as like a singer chanting the requiem of the beauty that had died in beauty. Claudius turned to her with his

usual glad greeting, "How now, sweet queen!"
  She exclaimed,

"One woe doth tread upon another's heels,
  So fast they follow. Your sister's drown'd,
    Laertes."

  He cried out, "Drown'd! O, where?"
  She told the story as it had been related to her,

"There is a willow grows aslant a brook,
  That shows his hoar leaves in the glassy stream;
  There with fantastic garlands did she come
  Of crow-flowers, nettles, daisies, and long purples;
  There, on the pendant boughs, her coronet weeds
  Clambering to hang, an envious sliver broke,
  When down her weedy trophies and herself
  Fell in the weeping brook. Her clothes spread
    wide,
  And, mermaid like, a while they bore her up;
  Which time she chanted snatches of old tunes,
  As one incapable of her own distress,
  Or like a creature native and indued
  Unto that element: but long it could not be
  Till that her garments, heavy with their drink,
  Pull'd the poor wretch from her melodious lay
  To muddy death."

At the question uttered by the brother, whether Ophelia had really been drowned, the Queen's composure gave way entirely. She merely sobbed,

"Drown'd, drown'd."

Laertes abruptly left the room. Claudius made immediate call upon his wife to be his companion, his confidante and his counsellor.

> "Let's follow, Gertrude;
> How much I had to do to calm his rage!
> Now fear I this will give it start again;
> Therefore let's follow."

He put his arm around her and drew her away with him. She trembled as she walked and he steadied her steps.

That evening Ophelia's aunt told the Queen, with some fullness, how Laertes, before his departure for France, had warned his sister of the danger she would run if she should any longer permit the royal Prince to pay her intimate attention. The aunt said that Ophelia had told her about it at the time.

"Madam," said the lady, "Laertes loved the Prince and he was loyal to him. He would not let himself think that his Highness meant to harm her, but he

[182]

knew marriage was almost impossible, and he did
know what sometimes happens when lovers find themselves in such a plight; and there might have been
heart-break for the poor maid even if there were not
ruin."

She spoke in more detail. Gertrude had, before
this, heard some rumors about the conduct of the
brother and father, but she now learned it all more
definitely.

"And Polonius,"—went on the aunt, "It nigh
broke his heart when he grew afraid that it was because he had not let the Prince see Ophelia that he
went mad."

As a result of this talk, a great wave of sympathetic
tenderness for Laertes flowed over Gertrude.

"I do not think," she said slowly, "that the Prince
had an evil purpose in his heart."

But she immediately made up her mind to do something herself to vindicate the honor of the dead girl.

The royal effort to conciliate Laertes was sufficiently successful. His thoughts were indeed, during the next few hours, concentrated on the death
of his sister, and the arrangements for her burial.
The church authorities held it to be doubtful whether
she had exactly committed suicide; but the doubt was

so great, that there was serious question what sort of funeral obsequies or burial could be granted her. Claudius took up her cause energetically, and sent instructions to two of the priests in charge of a church and cemetery nearby, to have a grave prepared in consecrated ground, and to arrange to give all possible religious solemnity to the act of interment. To make sure that his wishes were obeyed, he summoned a Church dignity, higher in authority than the local ones, to come to Elsinore. He coaxed or threatened that worthy and rather kindly old man, till he won from him a clerical endorsement of his own regal orders.

He could not, however, persuade this church official to attend the burial in person.

"Myself and the Queen will be there," said the King.

The representative of Rome answered, "My son, that were kindness in your Majesties. In me, it were to disregard the Christian rule, which is made not to soothe the heart of some single mourner, but to proclaim the doom of sinners and, thereby, to save other men from falling under condemnation."

Claudius was obliged to yield, and to accept a funeral programme, one portion of which practically declared Ophelia to have been a suicide, while the other part practically declared that she had met with an accidental death.

Claudius did the best he could to comfort Laertes in the matter, assuring him, in general terms that there should be respectful observance at the grave.

Having finished with Laertes and the priests, Claudius went to his wife's room. She was there alone, half·reclining on a thickly padded divan, over which were thrown several fur coverings. She wore a loose gown of silvery white samite, which came up close to her throat and down to her wrists. A long string of amber beads drooped from her neck nearly to her knees. Her hair floated on her shoulders. Its coloring harmonized with the glowing tints of the amber. She held a rosary and a diamond cross, which some crusader had brought to the Danish court from Italy.

The room was well illumined. She was in the centre of the light. A small golden bowl of steaming broth stood on a little table near her. The top of this table was of green malachite.

Gertrude raised her eyes to the King's face.

"You are weary, my lord," she said.

She rose, put down the rosary and cross, and made him take the place she had occupied among the furs on the divan. She took the bowl, seated herself on a hassock beside him, and coaxed him to drink the broth.

Claudius told her of his talk with Laertes and the priests.

"You are kind and thoughtful," she commented. Then she dropped her head upon the divan and cried, saying, "Oh, but my heart aches for it all. Poor little Ophelia!"

"No, no," whispered Claudius, "I can endure anything, except to see you weep."

She controlled herself, "I would not have you sad, because I mourn. Rest now. You need repose. Shall I sing to you?"

She had a rich contralto voice. Its tones beat softly at one's heart. She began to sing, and, involuntarily, because just then she could remember nothing else, she sang one of Ophelia's ballads,—

"Oh, bonny sweet Robin is all my joy."

Claudius watched her for a moment and then shut his eyelids.

Her beauty, her voice had done—I know not what, to his heart.

She did not look at him much while she was singing. She took up the cross again and she gazed absently at that and turned it in her fingers.

[186]

Gertrude of Denmark

Thoughts kept phrasing themselves in the mind of Claudius. Pitiless, soundless words, definite in meaning, fully expressive,—they went through his brain, as if pushed onward by some force, exterior to himself. They hurt his senses and not merely his soul, as they went. It was as though himself, yet not himself, were silently speaking thus to himself: "I deserve to be damned. I do not want to be damned."

Thrice, these words said themselves.

Not a quiver moved the face below or above the shut eyelids while this reiteration went on.

Then came other words, which seemed to be marshalled, yet by no summons of his own will, to argue against the first ones. Still, the verbal form was as though his own ego were making the argument.

"I am Denmark's chosen king. If Hamlet attack or accuse me, it breaks the State. It breaks *her* heart. Winter is coming. Civil war, famine, cold . . . *she* will cry. . . . The State and I together will go down. . . . If he—he only—die, she will grieve,—but not as in that other event.—Living, he is no real comfort to her. He is like his father. He has always strutted about, claiming that he knew better than she did, how his mother ought to think and act. Were he dead—she, knowing nothing—*knowing nothing*,—would love his memory—and—forget his madness. . . . It is a terrible road that stretches before me. . . . I must walk it, . . . I am Denmark's chosen king.—The past and the present constrain the future."

His whole face trembled. He bit back a groan that almost burst through his teeth.

The silent words went on,—trampling the substance of his brain.

"Oh, God—have mercy!—Oh God,—find another way. Let the lightning strike Hamlet dead tonight. —He—was—a—pretty child."

And all this while, she was caroling beside him. Not now was she singing of bonny, sweet Robin. She was chanting at random some fragments—of Latin hymns.

> "Ave maris stella
> Dei mater alma,"—

Gertrude's voice flowed on from the expression of ecstasy to that of tenderness in the next lines

> "Atque semper virgo
> Felix coeli porta."

Then came the old stanza ending

> "Corda voces et opera."

Here Claudius drew one gasping breath of pain.

Gertrude of Denmark

She gave him a quick glance, saw that his eyelids were still closed, and continued repeating

"Ave maris stella
Dei mater alma."—

The second line she chanted over and over

"Dei mater alma."

She turned her eyes away from him. She did it because of some strange instinct; but it was not an instinct of suspicion. It was rather that of protecting solicitude, a maternal sort of impulse which was restraining her from making too close an approach to one whom she felt to be weary or suffering. So, on she sang, alternating many strains and making brief pauses between them.

Claudius had not told her, that Hamlet was already back in Denmark.

As a consequence of instructions she had previously given, Gertrude was called suddenly away to the sick bed of a little child in the castle.

So soon as Claudius knew himself to be safely alone, his rigid immobility was broken by a physical paroxysm. His limbs, his body writhed in hysterical spasms.

This for some minutes. Then the movements grew feebler. He expelled his breath in faint moaning sounds.

A little longer, and the convulsions wholly ceased. He lay, in an attitude of exhaustion, as still as he might have lain in death.

CHAPTER XV

HORATIO, summoned to meet the Prince by his letter, had left Elsinore so speedily, after its receipt, that he had not learned of Ophelia's death. He found Hamlet disinclined to talk, at once, about what had befallen him since he had started on his embassy to England, or of what he now proposed to do. Therefore, Horatio knew only what Hamlet had written, namely that the ship, on which he had started, had encountered a pirate vessel; that there had been a fight; that Hamlet had boarded the attacking boat and had remained there, while his own Danish vessel had gone on towards England carrying Rosencrantz and Guildenstern. The pirates had treated Hamlet well and brought him back to Denmark. He had been wandering about the country, with these sailors, and had sent his letter by one or two of them to Elsinore.

With his accustomed tact, Horatio now simply waited till Hamlet should want to talk more freely of his own affairs, and neither of them knew what had happened on the bank of the fatal stream, where they, in boyhood, had often sat together, talking of Denmark's future and learning to love each other.

The day following their meeting, Hamlet proposed an apparently aimless stroll through odorous green fields. After an hour of walking, they came to a graveyard, in which they found two men digging a grave, and they stopped to talk with them. In this talk Hamlet's utterances were completely devoid of spiritual suggestion. They could not have been more so, being voiced in such a scene and at such a moment in his career, had he become entirely sceptical concerning the validity of any spiritual conceptions.

Small hillocks and little groves were scattered over the place, so that it was easy for the Prince and his friend to be quite near to any person and yet be hidden from all casual observance.

To such a covert, the two young men retired when the cemetery was entered by a stately procession. The King and Queen, many courtiers and two priests were in it, and all on foot. They came and stationed themselves, in proper order, around the ditch which the grave diggers had just opened.

Hamlet at once perceived that the "maimed rites" proclaimed that the corpse to be interred was that of a suicide. He recognized one of the mourners. "That is Laertes," he whispered to his companion, "a very noble youth." And then they both saw a curious scene and overheard a strange dialogue.

A garland had been borne in by pages before the bier. This garland was now hung high above the grave on a sort of maypole. Large heaps of flowers on two huge wicker trays were placed upon the ground, one at the head and the other at the foot of that awfully suggestive trench. There was some tolling of a bell, while the procession entered the yard of death and these few rites were being performed, and then that sound ceased. These observances were pretty enough, but, in that age, they were full of threatening portent because they were so simple and so few.

The brow of Laertes became corrugated. Was this the way his sister's body was to be huddled out of sight, her soul passed, from such life as he knew, into the ghastly ward of death? Although it was being done in the open sunshine, this funeral drama seemed to him to be an ironic sequel to that hideous farce of midnight burial, which had hidden his father's mortal part from human sight. Was no flesh sacred which was kindred to his own? He caught a glimpse of the clownish grave diggers, leaning on their spades at a little distance. One of them was grinning. He saw Yorick's empty skull lying in the grass where, though he himself knew it not, Prince Hamlet's hand had lately put it down with an exclamation of disgust.

Laertes felt as though the genius of life were dancing before him and wearing the cap and bells of mockery. The holy bell had ceased. The fool's bell was jingling in his ears.

"What ceremony else?" he demanded of the priest, —twice before he got an answer.

That answer, when it came, was more shocking to his hearing and his heart than even the meagre burial rites had been. The priest bluntly proclaimed the ordinary doom of the suicide in contrast with, what he held to be, the present leniency in its enforcement which had been the result of the King's instructions. He said,

"Her obsequies have been as far enlarg'd
As we have warrantise: her death was doubtful;
And, but that great command o'er sways the order,
She should in ground unsanctified have lodg'd
Till the last trumpet; for charitable prayers,
Shards, flints, and pebbles should be thrown on her:
Yet here she is allow'd her virgin crants,
Her maiden strewments, and the bringing home
Of bell and burial."

Horror crept over Laertes,—horror of the priest,

horror of his creed, horror of him as a man. Shards
and flints thrown over Ophelia's body—not prayers
breathed above it! He persisted, "Must there be no
more done?"

The impassive voice of authority made reply,

> "No more be done;
> We should profane the service of the dead
> To sing a requiem and such rest to her
> As to peace-parted souls."

A nerve broke in Laertes. Was the denial of
honor to be eternal? He clenched his hands, but he
controlled his voice, "Lay her i' the earth," he
commanded;—

> "And from her fair and unpolluted flesh
> May violets spring!"

He turned upon the black robed dignitary,

> "I tell thee, churlish priest,
> A ministering angel shall my sister be,
> When thou liest howling."

By this time, Hamlet had grasped the meaning of
what he saw and heard. He turned white and muttered low, but so that the words came to Horatio's
ear, "What, the fair Ophelia!"

Gertrude of Denmark

The Queen came forward to the brink and dropped flowers into the grave, saying in a choked voice,

"Sweets to the sweet; farewell."

Then after a pause, in a clearer, more resolute tone, still looking down, as though addressing the dead girl, but speaking with full intent that everyone present should hear what she said, Gertrude of Denmark pronounced the words that, as she believed, would stifle all future wonder whether Ophelia had surrendered her maidenly honor before she lost her life.

"I hoped thou shouldst have been my Hamlet's wife;
I thought thy bride-bed to have deck'd, sweet maid,
And not to have strew'd thy grave."

She stepped back among her waiting ladies and, standing behind two of them and covering her face with a veil, she had slight cognizance of what happened for two or three minutes.

Comforting as had been the Queen's words, noble and tender as was her gesture, Laertes had hardly taken in their purport, because of the passion that was growing torrential within him. He had heard the voices of earth and hell,—they were still pounding in his ears; he could not hear the voice of mercy and love.

The moment the Queen had withdrawn, a thought of Hamlet rushed upon him. He cried aloud,—yet not with stormy utterance,

> "O, treble woe,
> Fall ten times treble on that cursed head
> Whose wicked deed thy most ingenious sense
> Depriv'd thee of!"

Laertes was never known, after his return to Denmark, to refer plainly to the possible connection of Ophelia's lunacy with Hamlet's courtship. Outwardly and verbally, he seemed to accept the theory that the slaughter of her father was the cause of her sickness. Perhaps he felt that his sister's case was one of those, in which even to mention a love affair is to cast a doubt upon a woman's honor.

Now when he had spoken the sentences just given, Laertes suddenly addressed those dread masters of ceremony, the grinning grave diggers, "Hold off the earth awhile, till I have caught her once more in mine arms."

He hurled himself into the open fosse where the body of Innocence lay dead.

He broke into hysterical sobs. He felt that he

was holding her back for a moment from an unrighteous hell. He cried out,

"Now pile your dust upon the quick and dead,
Till of this flat a mountain you have made
To o'ertop old Pelion or the skyish head
Of blue Olympus."

Then another mad young man pushed his way through the crowd.

And which was the madder, and which had the more cause to be mad, who shall say?

This one strode to the edge of the ditch, demanding,

"What is he whose grief
Bears such an emphasis? Whose phrase of sorrow
Conjures the wandering stars, and makes them stand
Like wonder-wounded hearers? This is I,
Hamlet the Dane!"

He sprang lightly into the trench and stood close staring into the eyes of Ophelia's brother.

The hand of Laertes went straight to Hamlet's throat, "The devil take thy soul," he said.

Yet although he had that compelling hold upon the Prince, he did not exert any violent pressure, for

Hamlet was able to make quite a lengthy speech to this effect:

"Thou pray'st not well.
I prithee, take thy fingers from my throat;
For, though I am not splenetive and rash,
Yet have I something in me dangerous,
Which let thy wisdom fear. Hold off thy hand!"

Both men indeed showed marvellous self-control for a moment. Then Laertes dropped his hand from its vantage place, and suddenly, each man seemed loosed, as from a restraining leash, and grappled with the other in more violent but less immediately deadly fashion.

By this time Gertrude had become aware that something was happening and she returned to the King's side, near the grave, and saw her son struggling with his antagonist.

Claudius cried out, "Pluck them asunder."

The attendants called, "Gentlemen," and Gertrude's voice penetrated through the confused mass of expostulation and command.

"Hamlet, Hamlet!" she cried.

The two young men were dragged apart, and both of them came out of the grave and stood at a short distance from each other, till Hamlet spoke again,

"Why, I will fight with him upon this theme
Until my eyelids will no longer wag."

"O my son, what theme?" asked his mother.
"I lov'd Ophelia," returned Hamlet.

"Forty thousand brothers
Could not, with all their quantity of love,
Make up my sum,"

then glaring at the brother he demanded, "What wilt thou do for her?"

The quality of this speech was calculated to convince anew both the King and Queen that they were dealing with insanity.

"O, he is mad, Laertes," said Claudius, and Gertrude entreated the son of Polonius, "For love of God, forbear him."

Laertes respected her prayer and made no movement to renew the contest. He remained motionless and looked fixedly at Hamlet while the Prince let out a flood of words. Laertes, on the other hand, had not spoken since, ten minutes previously, Hamlet had leaped into the grave and he had taken the intruder by the throat, with the ejaculation, "The devil take thy soul." He maintained silence now and continued to do so, even when Hamlet accused him of "mouthing and ranting."

" 'Swounds, show me what thou'lt do:
Woo't weep? woo't fight? woo't fast? woo't tear
    thyself?
Woo't drink up eisel? eat a crocodile?
I'll do't. Dost thou come here to whine?
To outface me with leaping in her grave?
Be buried quick with her, and so will I:
And, if thou prate of mountains, let them throw
Millions of acres on us, till our ground,
Singeing his pate against the burning zone,
Make Osa like a wart! Nay, an thou'lt mouth,
I'll rant as well as thou!"

Still that silent hostile gaze from Laertes. But here Gertrude grew afraid that he would endure no more, and she went directly up and taking both his hands, which courtesy forbade him to withdraw, she made her plea in behalf of her son:

"This is mere madness:
And thus awhile the fit will work on him;
Anon, as patient as the female dove,
When that her golden couplets are disclos'd,
His silence will sit drooping."

As though the fit had passed, Hamlet turned, after this, to Laertes with something like an apology, thereby seeming to prove the correctness of his mother's diagnosis of his case. He made a tentative advance towards reconciliation, but still he spoke as if it were Laertes, who had been insulting and outraging him, demanding

> "Hear you, sir;
> What is the reason that you use me thus?"

Gertrude gasped at hearing this. "Has he forgot," she thought, "that, though it were by mistake, still it was he who killed the father of Laertes."

Laertes probably remembered it. At any rate he made no answer but, with his lips forming an inarticulate word to the Queen and almost bending his knee in saluting apology to her, he managed to get his hands free from the clasp of her fingers.

Perhaps he had a thought just then which connected Hamlet's wooing, as well as the killing of her father, with his sister's madness. Certainly, it is not likely that Hamlet's boastful willingness, whether uttered in frenzy or satire, to drink vinegar or even to eat a crocodile, to show his love, impressed Ophelia's brother very pleasantly at that moment.

Hamlet went on a little piteously, "I loved you ever."

Laertes, still speechless, turned on his heels away. Whereat the Prince, so finely and so boldly condemned, muttered,

> "But 'tis no matter;
> Let Hercules himself do what he may,
> The cat will mew, and dog will have his day."

Then he walked alone from the throng into the nearest thicket. Claudius sent Horatio to look after him. He spoke a word to Laertes, and then he begged "Good Gertrude, set some watch over your son," added a kindly promise to place a monument over Ophelia's grave, and said something about patience and "an hour of quiet" yet to be.

Laertes spoke no word.

CHAPTER XVI

AMBITION and love have nobility in their ingredients, and even hatred may have some lofty element in its composition. These had been the main passions which had moved Claudius in his progress towards crime, until after he had killed his brother. For some weeks now, a fouler passion had possessed him, a mad desire to protect himself. This fear had driven him down to the low level, on which he stood, when he poured a base alloy into the eager young soul of Laertes, and recast it in the mould of treachery. He was, however, destined to spawn, from his agony of self-love, a still viler deed.

The Prince went quietly from the graveyard and took up his old quarters in the castle. Gertrude slept peacefully that night, and her first waking thought, in the morning, was "Hamlet is at home."

On this day Horatio and the Prince chose the great hall to walk and talk in. They felt securer from espionage in its vast spaces than they might have done in a smaller room. They moved arm in arm up and down in the middle, keeping themselves well away from alcoves and wall curtains which might conceal listeners and spies.

Here and then, Hamlet told his friend that, in the night during the voyage to England, he got possession of the package of sealed orders, which Rosencrantz and Guildenstern had been instructed to deliver to the English authorities. He opened it and learned that it carried a request, from King Claudius, that he himself should be put to death immediately upon his arrival. He took away the document, wrote out another in proper form, stamped it with his father's signet ring, and put this forged paper in the place of the original one. He paused in the middle of some irrelevant and flippant discourse about his handwriting, over which he dallied, perhaps because he shrank from telling exactly what he had done. In this pause, he asked Horatio if he really wanted to know what was the order which he had forged.

Horatio said he did; whereupon Hamlet, after some more circumlocution, let out the facts. He had demanded in the name of Denmark's king, that his English ally should put the bearers of the despatch "to sudden death, no shriving time allowed."

It had been one of the chief counts against his uncle, that that man had put King Hamlet to death,

"no shriving time allowed." Hamlet had once resolved upon a scheme of vengeance which should
send his uncle to his final reckoning, "no shriving
time allowed."

He had now progressed so far on the road towards
extreme depravity, as to execute a similarly fiendish
purpose in relation to the comrades of his boyhood.
To insure his own safety, he had needed only to write
a despatch commending himself to England's kindness. Also if he had, as some commentators think,
planned that the vessel, on which he had been sent,
should be attacked by pirates, who were to connive at
his escape and let the ship go on carrying his companions to England, there was still no reason why, for
his own sake, he should give instructions for the execution of his old school fellows, concerning whom he
had once prattled so affectionately to his mother.
But he had grown to dislike them because they
watched him, and because he knew that they had been
told to do so.

A cat may look upon a king, but it was to incur
the death penalty to look at Hamlet, even as a duly
constituted guardian.

If Hamlet were sane, the only conclusion can be
that he had a peculiar disposition; in that he tried to
make people believe him insane, and yet he was ir-

ritated with everybody, from Ophelia down, whom he succeeded in making accept that belief.

Horatio was evidently slightly shocked by what Hamlet did. But he apparently recovered speedily. His conduct had the appearance of sycophancy. Probably however it was not really quite that. Hamlet's personality always dazzled and bewildered him. He could not see things pertaining to the Prince in their true color. He could not entertain thoughts in opposition to Hamlet.

Another incident, in this interview between Hamlet and his confidant, must be regretfully noted. He characterized his mother by a coarser word than he had ever previously used in his soliloquies, or his conferences with Horatio. This increasing unreserve marked the increasing deterioration of his nature.

He did not speak a doubtful word;—he used a phrase which was tantamount to a statement that his mother had committed adultery.

There have been sons who would have cast the mantle of silence over a mother's actual sin and shame. This one had no such filial impulse to hide even the mere suspicion, which the Ghost had thrown down at his feet. He lifted it up, stuffed it, clothed it with a fabric woven in his brain and showed the puppet, to another man, declaring it to be the true image of his own mother. Alas for "Hamlet, the Dane!"

He also disclosed, more plainly than he ever had before, his feeling about the fact that his uncle, and not he, had obtained the grant of the throne. Counting up the things which Claudius had done against himself, the Prince said, "He . . . popp'd in between the election and my hopes."

After all this strange medley of serious and flippant discourse, Hamlet proceeded to ask Horatio what he thought was his own right and duty to do about Claudius. He said,

"Is't not perfect conscience,
To quit him with this arm? and is't not to be damn'd,
To let this canker of our nature come
In further evil?"

Horatio did not answer this perplexing question. He merely remarked that the fate of Rosencrantz and Guildenstern must shortly be made known to Claudius by message from England. Hamlet admitted that this must be so, and then went on to say that he was "very sorry" for the way he had behaved to Laertes at the grave. He averred that he had begun to feel sympathy for him, because he, like himself, had lost a father. "I'll court his favours," he said, "but, sure, the bravery of his grief did put me in a towering passion."

Nobody but himself could be permitted by this gigantic egotist to have "a towering passion" in relation to aught which concerned him.

While this colloquy was proceeding Hamlet's enemies were arranging for the projected challenge and duel.

Laertes produced the poisoned foil. Two cups of wine were to be placed beside the King at the time of the meeting. He engaged to drop poison into one of them while the encounter should be in progress. The plan was, that should the fencing bout conclude without Laertes having succeeded in pricking Hamlet with the envenomed foil, the King should call upon his victorious nephew to drink with him, and the fatal cup should be the one which the young man would naturally lift.

Laertes felt a little averse to this treacherous mode of compassing what he held to be the ends of justice. He would have preferred an open attack, and even the cutting of his adversary's "throat in a church." But he saw that the reasons were very cogent which his sovereign had for desiring a more secret method. The King urged it, until compliance took the aspect of a duty connected with allegiance. And the injuries which he had to avenge were so enormous! "A noble father lost, a sister driven into desperate terms." Her eternal salvation endangered in consequence. Of course he feared that. He had defied the priest in the cemetery. But still his mind and his heart were both under the influence of the traditional belief of the period in churchly pronouncement. His soul was sick with horror. Ophelia in Hell . . . and his own grief mocked and jeered at beside her grave.

Laertes consented.

CHAPTER XVII

A COURTIER, Osric by name, brought to Hamlet a challenge to fence with Laertes. He was told that his uncle had wagered six Barbary horses against six French rapiers that he would beat Laertes.

Hamlet, rather against Horatio's wish, said he would make trial of his fencing skill at once with his antagonist there in the hall.

A second messenger came to tell him that the King and Queen were coming to see the sport.

"In happy time," said Hamlet.

"The Queen," continued this nobleman, "desires you to use some gentle entertainment to Laertes before you fall to play."

"She well instructs me," answered Hamlet thoughtfully.

This young nobleman was fortunate enough to obtain speech with the Queen before she was to descend with the King to the hall. Her eyes were lighted. Osric was with her, and he had been telling her that the Prince had treated him very courteously.

During Osric's interview with Hamlet, the Prince

had really been, most of the time, either mocking him
openly or sneering at him aside to Horatio. Osric
had been uncomfortably aware of all this, and was
annoyed by it, but he had deemed it to be both wise
and dutiful in himself to keep his temper as best he
could. Hamlet had requested him to waive the ceremony of removing his hat, and the young fellow re-
ported this to Gertrude as a gracious and courteous
action. He did so because he knew it would please
her. He colored his narrative to Hamlet's advantage.
Osric followed the instinct of the courtier; that is true,
but he was also and more urgently prompted by the
fact that he felt a boyish adoration for the Queen.
She was the chosen lady of his troubadour sort of
worship.

It was a worship, which put on the guise of affected
and ridiculous love, merely because Osric had heard
that thus to simulate was the fashion among poetic
soldiers in Southern climes. In reality his feeling
for the Queen was a filial passion kindled by a pure
and ennobling idealism.

Gertrude had only a tolerant liking for Osric himself, but she was as happy, because she thought that
Hamlet had made him happy, as though she were
delighted on Osric's own account.

"Did he smile on you?" she asked, "then you must

be glad, for the Prince's smile is one to gladden any heart. I wish I had seen how he looked—and how you did."

The newcomer added his report of the gracious speech which His Highness had made, in commendation of her message, betokening, as it seemed, his full sympathy with her desire that friendship should subsist between himself and the son of the slain Polonius.

When she heard this, joy came into Gertrude's heart like a sublimated stimulant. She was aware indeed that sorrow had been moving close behind her, —that sorrow was still present at her side, but perhaps that consciousness only made her more exultantly glad to receive this entrance of joy into her house of life.

In less than half an hour more, the sovereigns and their train of attendants came in and took their allotted stations.

The pageant so quickly staged was only a little less brilliant than that one in which these same men and women had figured, on the evening when professional players had enacted the mock tragedy, whose issue had been real to soul and body both.

Eager and listless countenances were here and jewels shone over laces and velvets now as then.

One face was missing though, the face of a girl with sad eyes, white cheeks and tightly compressed lips.

As the King and Queen seated themselves Claudius had his right hand inside the breast of his scarlet tunic. He drew it out and laid it lightly on his wife's shoulder. She did not appear to notice his touch. He shuddered;—took his hand away and put it back inside his breast. After a while, he brought it forth again and let it lie closed upon his knee. He now held a tiny package shut in on his palm by his fingers.

Gertrude turned toward him then and said in an affectionate tone,

"You are shivering, my lord. It is cold in this hall, as that nice lad Osric told me that Hamlet said it was when he bade him not to stand uncovered. Are you chilly? Shall I send for another robe?"

Claudius shook his head negatively, but she rearranged the wrap that he had around him.

She saw that he was holding something. She thought it was a pearl which she had heard that he intended to dissolve in wine out of compliment to her son, if he should be the victor.

Gertrude was feeling very satisfied just then with Claudius. He had seemed to her to be very good natured about Hamlet's sudden return to Denmark of which he had merely said to her:

"Hamlet boarded the pirate ship like a brave man attacking an enemy. It was a rash deed. He became their prisoner. But it turned out well enough. They dared not ill-treat a Danish prince, and they set him free on our shores."

In reply to her question about the English mission, Claudius had answered carelessly.

"Oh, the other envoys took the papers on to England. Hamlet can follow on another ship if it shall seem best."

So Gertrude still considered Hamlet to be an ambassador and was content, sitting beside Claudius.

She reached out her left hand, with the wedding ring upon it, and gave a fleeting feather-like caressing touch to the kingly fingers that held that little something. Then, as the moment had arrived for Hamlet's first action, she turned swiftly from her sovereign and husband to gaze at her boy, her Prince.

Hamlet went straight across the intervening space to Laertes. They were nearly of the same height, though Hamlet was the more heavily built and the older of the two, and he panted a little when he began to speak. Laertes looked steadily at him. However

Hamlet may have conceived the situation, Laertes considered himself to be confronting the man who had dug two graves and had cast therein, the innocent forms of that old age and that youth which were nearest to his own reverent duty.

Hamlet spoke at length and aloud for all the assembly to hear, and flatly gave the lie to everything he had said to his mother on the subject, declaring unequivocally that he had been insane when he killed Polonius, and therefore should be acquitted by the son of all blame in the matter. "What I have done," he said, "I here proclaim was madness."

Gertrude listened to this with satisfaction, because she believed that he had now come to realize the truth of his former condition,—and that meant that he had suddenly, that very day indeed, recovered.

Laertes let Hamlet talk a long time, before he relaxed the severity of his demeanor enough to reply. Meanwhile Gertrude watched both the young men with ever growing sympathy for her son, and with a greater gladness because she thought that now he was showing a finer spirit than the other was.

At last Laertes told the lie and made the false promises which constituted his acceptance of Hamlet's plea for friendliness.

The foils were given to the combatants, Gertrude

was pleased to hear Claudius express his desire that Hamlet should win.

One moment of still deeper joy was vouchsafed her.

As the two young men moved to their places on the floor, Hamlet turned his beautiful head, looked at her, lifted his left hand to his lips, kissed it and waving it, bowed a salute.

The fencing began. She watched it with a smile. She saw her darling now, as one restored to health, lovely in his powerful manhood, returned to Denmark clothed with the dignity of an ambassador, . . . her son, . . . her perfect creation . . . and he loved her . . . rapture of raptures, he loved her once more!

The moments passed. She saw, in a mystical kind of vision, only grace and glory contending for greater glory.

There came a pause in the combat. She heard Hamlet breathing hard.

She called, "Here, Hamlet, take my napkin, rub thy brows."

She took a cup of wine from a table between herself and the King.

She stood erect and her clear sweet voice pealed through the hall.

Gertrude of Denmark

"The Queen carouses to thy fortune, Hamlet."

She felt the King clutch at her gown. She heard him gasp, "Gertrude, do not drink."

She turned a laughing, unseeing glance upon him, and with a gesture of infinite courtesy, she said, "I will, my lord; I pray you, pardon me."

And then, to save himself from immediate exposure, he did not snatch away the cup into which he had lately dropped the pellet prepared for Hamlet.

She drank.

Her son called to her in response to her toast, "I dare not drink yet, madam; by and by."

She uttered an absurdly tender prayer to the flushed and heated swordsman, "Come, let me wipe thy face,"—actually received an answering smile from him as he turned back to renew the combat and then, blushing for her ridiculous show of solicitude, the Queen of Denmark stood still beside the King.

She did not see the King's face. It was stiffened with agony. Yet he continued to make brave effort; and she again heard him loudly proclaim his confidence in Hamlet's prowess.

Laertes pricked Hamlet with his poisoned weapon. A violent scuffle ensued, in the course of which, the foils changed hands, and Hamlet, in his excitement, stabbed Laertes so deeply with the envenomed blade,

[218]

that the wound would doubtless have been mortal even had all the poison been rubbed off in the prick given to himself.

The violence of Hamlet's thrust is attested by the fact that Laertes died many minutes before he did.

When the King saw that both men were wounded, he cried out, "Part them; they are incens'd."

Laertes was staggering to the earth, but Hamlet hearing the King's command shouted angrily to his sinking opponent, "Nay, come, again."

Meanwhile Gertrude had sunken into her chair. Osric, who had been acting as umpire, was the first in the throng nearest to the fencers, to see what was happening to her.

"Look to the Queen there, ho!" he cried madly, then recognizing his helplessness he did not rush forward to her side.

Some women gently drew Gertrude on to cushions laid upon the floor.

Horatio, with his eyes turned only on the swordsmen, exclaimed "They bleed on both sides," and, laying a hand on Hamlet's shoulder, said, "How is it, my lord?"

Osric stooped down above Hamlet's fallen antagonist and with trembling lips asked tenderly, "How is it, Laertes?"

Gertrude of Denmark

In a moment more Gertrude heard Hamlet's demanding question, "How does the queen?"

She no longer knew who was near or who was far in the confusion around her, but she did hear Claudius stammer forth his abominable lie, "She swoons to see them bleed."

Some sort of awareness came to her, "No, no," she groaned, "the drink, the drink—"

She thought she felt her son's arms around her. The supreme passion of her life asserted itself. "O, my dear Hamlet," she whispered. She moaned again, "The drink, the drink,—I am poisoned," she said.

Then a mother died.

Osric was still kneeling apart from the group around the dead Queen. He hid his face in his hands. His body shook with dry sobs.

Hamlet, learning instantly not only that there had been poison in the cup whence the Queen had drunk but on the blade which he held, called out: "The point envenomed too! Then venom to thy work!" and stabbed the King. Not satisfied with the possible effect of his thrust, he caught up the cup, crying,

"Here, thou incestuous, murtherous, damned Dane,
Drink off this potion! Is thy union here?
Follow my mother."

Gertrude of Denmark

Those words were the last articulate human utterances that Claudius heard.

In Hamlet's history, this execution of vengeance was only an incident. It did not indicate a stage in the development of his soul or character. That came a moment later when he bent beside the dying Laertes.

EPILOGUE

SLOWLY did one of the mysteries, with which Gertrude's life was involved, reveal itself to me.

Hamlet was a monstrous egotist, who could question all things in the Universe, himself included, but who could not see the answers to his questions, because his egoism imposed itself like a tangible substance between the eyes of his mind and everything in the Universe, not excluding himself.

Therefore he became a spirit of doubt. Therefore it was that he became, mainly, incarnated Doubt.

Before he knew the facts, he doubted his uncle because, to a large extent, he had already divined the man's capacity for evil doing.

He doubted his mother after receiving provocation to a mistaken opinion.

At first, he believed emotionally in the Ghost. Later, he intellectually doubted that great It.

In one fatal midnight hour, he embraced the spirit of Revenge and blended its essence with the corrosive elements of Doubt.

After that, although he was still occasionally

stirred by the consciousness of the Ethical Necessities which control life, his moral deterioration had a progressive though slightly wavering growth.

Neither his mother's love nor Ophelia's at this juncture in his career, could check his wrongful course, because, on the whole, he desired to compass revenge rather than to execute justice; and also because he lacked the faith that would have prompted him either to forgive or to wish to be forgiven. And that sort of faith is needful for salvation.

All the moral convolutions in his soul were intertwisted with the tangle of his philosophical speculations. He had no clear and strong consciousness of the ethical verities.

Hamlet could trace the origin of the material in the spigot, that stopped the bung hole of a beer barrel, back to the grave, wherein had lain "the noble dust of Alexander." But the eyes of his mind saw only the movement of dust from the grave to the bung hole; his reason perceived only the way that the spigot had come into visible existence. Therefore he did not apprehend the realities around him.

He saw only the silliest and worst side of an old man, in whom there was no great harm and was much kindly good, and who bore a relation to Ophelia

which should have entitled him to respectful treatment from her lover.

He doubted Ophelia without the least valid excuse,
unless it be one to be too destitute of imaginative sympathy to realize that, in withdrawing herself from
him, she was doing merely what he would have re-
joiced to see his own sister do in her case.

He said that he had loved Laertes "ever." In reality, he gave no thought at all to him, till he felt himself affronted by the assumption of Laertes that he,
the brother, was by right the chief mourner beside
Ophelia's grave.

When he should have believed in Laertes and consulted him because he was Ophelia's natural guardian, Hamlet paid no attention to him. Later, when
Laertes had become his deadly enemy, his egotistic
vision of himself as Ophelia's lover, made him incapable of realizing that her brother might hate him
for being her destroyer. So he believed in Laertes
then and consented to fence with him. Yet, when he
remembered that Laertes was a son whose father had
been slain, the likeness to his own fate aroused in
him some little sympathetic impulse.

Hamlet had once loved two amiable boys. He
came to despise them out of his intellectual superi-

ority, to hate them and to murder them by proxy,
urged thereto by unjustified suspicion and revenge·
ful desire.

He clung to Horatio with a trustful affection, which
was never subjected to any crucial test, because there
was a temperamental harmony between them, and
also because Horatio admired him almost unreservedly.

Laertes, when dying, made confession of his guilt
as to the poisoning, and then Hamlet, knowing himself to be also death-stricken, heard the stiffening lips
of the son of Polonius murmur,

"Exchange forgiveness with me, noble Hamlet;
Mine and my father's death come not upon thee,
Nor thine on me."

Receiving thus, the free gift of unsolicited forgiveness from one whom he had injured much, Hamlet's
soul rose, as it were, on the wings of another's gener-
osity, and he answered, "Heaven make thee free of
it," and he added, "I follow thee."

Perhaps he consciously meant only that he was to
follow Laertes in the act of dying, but really he had
then begun to follow him spiritually, upward.

Yet in his own very last moment, this egotist's

thoughts were mainly occupied with anxious speculation about the reputation he would leave behind
him—

"Report me and my cause aright
  To the unsatisfied."
"O God!—Horatio, what a wounded name,
  Things standing thus unknown, shall live behind
      me!"
"Absent thee from felicity awhile,
  And in this harsh world, draw thy breath in pain,
  To tell my story."
". . . Tell him, with occurrents more and less,
  Which have solicited,—
  The rest is silence." . . . So be it.

The pine trees have fallen by my home, but still
they stand evergreen and beautiful, in the mystical
region where my spirit dwells apart.

In the shadow of those pines, however, one duty re-
mains to me. I must beg pardon of the phantom
Gertrude, since, in obeying her behest to tell her
story, I have been unable to gloss over her son's im-
perfections with inappropriate and unproved general-
ities of characterization, as most commentators have
done.

She would have been glad to have all his sins and

errors hidden from the world. Yet she possessed a righteous sense, which made her defend a person from false accusation, no matter what might be the consequence to the guilty one of such defense.

She showed this quality when, rather than permit Claudius to be blamed for a crime he had not committed, she risked the divulging to Laertes of the secret, which implicated Hamlet in the death of Polonius.

In a like spirit and in order to vindicate others, I have been impelled to write what I have seen to be the truth as to Hamlet's faults.

Such sad truth-telling is often the pre-requisite to the movement of art towards harmony.

Only through full knowledge of the sin can both that divine and human compassion develop, which will stay by the sinner till penitence shall come to him:—after which Mercy may seal the whole experience with the forgiveness which consecrates life.

NOW AT THE END THIS WORD

Love, merely as an unmoral emotion to be enjoyed, will save no man, and no world wherein men live. Else had Claudius been saved from both sin and ruin.

Gertrude of Denmark

The moral purpose must hold, control and direct all emotion in its action.

Is it on the whisper of Gertrude, the voice of Shakspeare or the breath of the evergreen pines that this final message is borne to my hearing?

APPENDIX

CAREFUL study of an unabridged edition of the play of "Hamlet" will, I think, yield to the reader may clues to the motives and feelings, which I have attributed to the various personages in this interpretative romance. Suggestions may also be found in the tragedy for some of the imagined incidents which I have interspersed among those which are drawn directly from the play.

The quotations are copied from Rolfe's edition. So much of the original text is, however, omitted from Rolfe's version, that, in order to appreciate my characterization either my rendition of character and motive must be accepted without question, or recourse must be had to an edition of the tragedy which has not been cut.

I think it proper to state here that, when I wrote nearly the whole body of this romance, I had read almost none of the criticisms of the play. The reading, upon which is founded much that I say in this appendix, has been done since I had essentially finished my story.

Gertrude of Denmark

At the time I wrote my account of the midnight interview between Gertrude and Hamlet, I did not know that some actress did once represent the mother as going towards the son with an affectionate gesture, just before he leaves her. I have also learned lately that the woman, who in this winter (1923–4) plays the Queen in Martin-Harvey's company, touches caressingly the hand in which Claudius holds the poison.

I have never seen a good performance of the tragedy of Hamlet. I once saw a rather poor one and I have forgotten most of its details. The psychological effect upon me of this experience was that, while writing my romance, I found myself inclined to rejoice that I was able to concentrate all my attention upon Shakspeare's text, undisturbed by the accompanying recollection of the way in which this or that actor had interpreted any portion of it. Nevertheless, I am also thankful that I have seen many great actors, men and women both, and many of the class only just below greatness. I seem to myself, thereby, to have imbibed into my imagination something of that quality with which the theatrical art alone can infuse the mind and soul of the student of life and literature. I feel that, in this special case, I have received the necessary artistic inspiration without coming under the spell of any one actor's personality. I did see Edwin Booth and Henry Irving each many times and Fechter once or twice, but no one of them as Hamlet. However, I once heard Irving say, as I sat beside him, that Edwin Booth represented the mystical, brooding element, in Hamlet's nature better than any one else whom he had ever seen.

Let me now proceed to tell briefly what I have tried to do and to avoid doing in the construction of this romance. I wish in this appendix also to contrast my critical opinions with those held by some other commentators and to compare theirs with each other. Thus, I hope to make plain to some extent the reason for the faith that is in me and which has controlled the effort that has gone into this story of Gertrude of Denmark.

An historical novelist may properly decide which actual facts he will use and which he will discard, in order to make his story move in the direction he desires. He may also manipulate facts and re-mould historical character to fit the need of his own imagination.

My task in fashioning this romance differed from that of the historical novelist, and my rights were different. I founded my work upon an already created literary production. Having chosen this mighty foundation for my small structure, I felt constrained to take the material furnished by the tragedy of "Hamlet" exactly as it is in the version which has been accepted as standard. I have treated this version as though it were an absolutely true historical narrative, but one with which I had not the historical novelist's privilege to tamper. I have incorporated, into my romance, the dialogue of Shakspeare's drama as frankly as I might have taken such speech from a stenographer's report of actual conversation, treating it as one which I had no right to alter in order to harmonize it with my individual fancies as to the idiosyncrasies of the persons concerned. I have taken no liberties with the text itself. But I have felt entitled to give what seemed to me reasonable interpretations of the actions and speeches provided by the drama.

There are passages in the text which can be variously interpreted. As to them I have chosen or originated the interpretation which I preferred. And my preference has been to interpret speeches and incidents with due regard to the proportionate value of the significance thus assigned them to that of the larger body of the entire work.

In my romance I have interpolated the scenes

drawn from the drama with imaginary ones, taking care that the dialogue and the incidents in them should not be inconsistent with my own conception of the personages in the tragedy.

I have nowhere assumed that persons in the play could not, or ought not to, have done or said what they are represented as doing or saying, because I should have liked it better if they had not done or said those things. Thus, apropos of Hamlet's declaration to Laertes that he had killed Polonius in a fit of insanity, I do not say with Dr. Johnson, "I wish Hamlet had made some other defense; it is unsuitable to the character of a brave or a good man to shelter himself under a falsehood." Dr. Johnson transcends his function as a critic in saying this, and arrogates to himself the right that the preacher or the essayist has in commenting upon the character of a real person.

It is not the business of a critic, in discussing the character portraiture in a work of the imagination, to "wish" things like the above. It would, in this case, be a critic's business to consider whether Shakspeare meant that Hamlet had come to believe that he had been insane, and so had spoken what he believed to be the truth, or whether he meant to represent him as telling a deliberate lie. The critic might go on also to discuss the question how much excuse the incidents of the drama offered for such a lie, and thence proceed to the further inquiry whether Shakspeare intended to represent Hamlet as being either a brave or a good man.

Seymour gives it as his opinion, that the whole passage is an interpolation; and he states his reason for so thinking to be that "the falsehood contained in it is too ignoble." Too ignoble for whom?—too ignoble for Shakspeare to have imagined? A theory of interpolation, to be accepted, must be supported by historical or literary reasons affecting the text itself.

The Reverend C. E. Moberley uses the imagination of an historical novelist, not the discrimination of a literary critic, when he says quite calmly, that had not the pirate vessel attacked Hamlet's ship the very day after he had forged the orders for the execution of Rosencrantz and Guildenstern, "we may conclude with safety that Hamlet's *kindly nature* would have cancelled the letters." (The italics are mine.)

Apparently, in the opinion of this reverend gentleman, the Prince's "kindly nature" required time to develop. How much? one wonders. George Eliot's theory is to the effect that, what a man does quickly, in a sudden emergency, bears witness to the nature of his previous moral habit.

A critic, who talks about the cancellation of forged documents by a "kindly nature" rather than by the man who possesses it, is perhaps unworthy of much serious attention. But Moberley is largely quoted by both Rolfe and Furness, and he may be ordinarily respected as an authority upon Shakspearean characterization, if not upon the use of the English language.

The pertinent question is, not how slowly did Hamlet's "kindly nature" usually wake up from slumber, but did Shakspeare create a Hamlet endowed with such a nature. The first evidence, which Shakspeare offers on this subject, may be found in a speech he puts into Hamlet's mouth before the Ghost has excited him by revealing to him his uncle's guilt. Hamlet then says of the day on which his mother had married his uncle, "Would I had met my dearest foe in Heaven or ever I had seen that day, Horatio."

Of course, this is merely an exclamation, but the exclamations, which leap from a man's lips, are apt to be indicative of his temper; and this one certainly suggests a tendency towards vindictive impulse.

Does Hamlet's rudeness to Polonius smack either of kindliness or instinctive courtesy? Was his mockery of Osric's mannerisms amiable? And was not his "towering passion" towards Laertes beside the dead body of Ophelia, more symptomatic of brutality than of kindliness?

Hazlitt says "Hamlet is the most amiable of misanthropes." Dr. Conolly, on the other hand, says, "The diffusion of the element of tenderness over the whole of Hamlet's character, however skilfully effected on the stage, is an unauthorized departure from the delineation of his character by Shakspeare." Victor Hugo says, "Hamlet is this sinister thing a possible parricide." The context shows that Hugo means a possible matricide.

This comment leads straight to the consideration of the speech in which Hamlet says that he is in a mood to "drink hot blood," and then reminds himself that he must not kill his mother. Hunter thinks it strange that the Poet deemed it necessary to make Hamlet say he would not do what Orestes (Electra assisting) did to Clytemnestra, because "to be sure" this Hamlet would not do such a thing. This remark may be dismissed quietly as an assumption on the part of Hunter that he was much more familiar with Shakspeare's intentions in the characterization of Hamlet than the dramatist was himself.

Of the Gertrude shown in Shakspeare's final version of the play (much changed from older ones), Hunter says, she "had done nothing to deserve it (death); it is not even insinuated against her that she was acquainted with the manner of her former husband's death. Her offence was marrying too soon, and in addition to this that her second husband was brother to the first."

I cannot wholly agree with Hunter. I think Hamlet did insinuate a charge against Gertrude of complicity in the murder of his father, when he said, "Almost as bad, good mother, as kill a king and marry with his brother." But he dropped this insinuation almost as soon as he had uttered it. Hunter is right, however, so far as the rest of the tragedy is concerned.

It is a curious phenomenon also in the portraiture, that no living person is shown as suspecting Claudius of the murder. Horatio, merely, imbibes Hamlet's belief in the Ghost's assertion, and having imbibed it, naturally draws the same conclusion as the Prince does, from the behavior of the King in the theatre. He initiates no such idea. The rabble revolt against Claudius in excitement caused by the death of Polonius. They were not at all disturbed on account of King Hamlet's sudden decease.

We know that the Ghost's charge of murder is true,

because Claudius confesses it in soliloquy and in prayer. No confession or soliloquy substantiates the Ghostly insinuation of adultery against Gertrude. Nobody suspects it, since again Horatio merely does not contradict Hamlet when he speaks of it as a fact. Among the critics, however, Swinburne seems to stand, if not with Hunter, still in a neutral attitude. He says simply that the character of Gertrude is left uncertain in the Folio version of the play.

The critics have generally denounced Gertrude's second marriage as sinful in its very nature. It is rather absurd to echo Hamlet so completely as to this. Such an opinion certainly has been very dominant in some ages and some countries. It is doubtful, however, whether it was ever so universally an accepted belief as to make it certain that Shakspeare intended that such a mountain of odium should be heaped upon her, as writers have been piling up for centuries. In this connection, it may be noted, that the Roman Catholic Church upheld the marriage of Katharine to Henry the Eighth. And certainly, Shakspeare, however Anglican he may have been personally, did not represent Katharine as a loathsome creature in his drama on that subject, and he did permit Henry's courtiers to jeer at the King's pretence of scruple.

Gertrude of Denmark

Who, moreover, is going to insist that it is actually sinful to marry in "haste"? It is merely indecorous to do so, if there be not excellent reason for speedy action,—and sometimes there is excellent reason.

The critical comment upon Ophelia is a strange medley. Much of it seems to be inspired by each writer's own particular bias of opinion towards the function of maidenhood in the life of the world. Some utterance has been clearly but irrelevantly influenced by earlier composition than that of the Folio.

Hamlet's own attitude towards her, should not, in my opinion, be taken as a necessarily correct indication of what Shakspeare meant to be considered her character.

Hamlet's ferocious outbursts at her in the scene where she offers back his gifts, are made by some actors to alternate with tenderness in speech and action. His ferocity is explained by representing him as suddenly catching sight of Polonius and Claudius overlooking the interview. He is supposed to conclude that Ophelia may herself be a spy, and that she tells him a deliberate lie when, in answering his disconcerting question, she says that her father is at home. Grant White writes of this interpretation,

"There is no warrant for the opinion that Hamlet had discovered that the King and Polonius were overhearing."

As for Ophelia's assertion that her father was at home, I find no certain evidence, in the text, that she did know that he was not there. The idea, that she knew definitely that he and the King were then watching Hamlet and herself, is based on the supposition that she had heard everything said by them, before they and the Queen had left her in the lobby. It seems more likely that, during those preparatory moments, she had stayed deferentially at a little distance from her elders and betters, and consequently did not learn that there were to be "lawful espials" to the coming scene.

If, however, Ophelia did hear enough to learn that guardianship was to be provided her in the arranged interview, she may well have been confused by Hamlet's behavior into momentary forgetfulness where, in all this dreary world, her father was just then. In that case, her answer to Hamlet's demand "Where is your father?" would be a mechanical utterance of no mental or moral significance whatever.

At worst it was only a frightened lie. Perhaps there was not even a taint of cowardice in it. It may have been inspired by a sense of duty. She may have felt that it would be wrong to betray her father and her sovereign to this frenzied young man: —and would she not have been justified in so feeling? It must be remembered that Ophelia is represented as really believing that Hamlet was insane. Is it not an accepted opinion that there are circumstances in which it is right and wise to tell a falsehood to a maniac? Did Shakspeare necessarily intend to make Ophelia either culpably false or weak?

Critics, enamoured of Hamlet, have dubbed the persons "spies" and "sponges" who tried to learn what was actually the matter with him. Is it probable that Shakspeare, who was dramatic if he were anything in characterization, intended to convey the idea that only despicable people would exercise over an insane prince a watchful guardianship? In real life, these commentators would doubtless see that a man and especially a prince, who becomes insane or who wilfully puts on "an antic disposition," should be the subject of careful observation both by his responsible kindred and by the servants and rulers of the State. That Claudius had his own special and evil motive for investigating Hamlet's condition does not alter the fact that, as king and uncle, he was performing his duty in making that investigation; and Shakspeare makes it evident, to any careful student of the text, that Claudius and Gertrude did not employ "sponges" or "spies" but worthy assistants to help them in their task.

Tieck is one of the foremost among the critics who are unsympathetic towards Ophelia. He is convinced that she had "yielded all to Hamlet" before her father and brother attempted to stop the intimacy. He considers her so jaunty about her own degradation, that when Laertes bids her think of Hamlet's love as "a violet in the youth of primy nature," she, knowing how far things had gone, *"naïvely and smilingly* asks, 'No more but so?' " (The italics are mine.) Tieck moreover cannot imagine how "an innocent girl" could speak to her brother as she does urging him not to do wrong himself. This inability of Tieck's seems to be the result of that mental feebleness which is engendered by the habit of believing that ignorance provides maidenhood with the only atmosphere wherein purity can flourish. Tieck says Hamlet treats Ophelia "without that respect which she appears to him to have long before forfeited."

Pries thinks that Hamlet's indelicate speeches to Ophelia, in the theatre, were made to let Claudius realize that this girl was the Prince's particular property and to warn his Majesty not to trespass. The claim of this theory to validity rests on the improb-

Gertrude of Denmark

able supposition that Hamlet shouted his remarks loud enough for them to be heard by the King and Gertrude and other folks! Pries admits that this interpretation has no warrant furnished by the text.

Steevens, probably trying to excuse Hamlet, thinks that similar talk was common in the English world of Shakspeare's period. Maybe it was,—but it is not "common" in Shakspeare's dramatic world. It is indeed unprecedented there. There are indelicacies in Shakspeare, but they are not uttered by his high-bred men to women whom they love. Hamlet is the only young man in the whole Shakspearean drama, whose education and station entitle him to be called a gentleman, who says vile things to a maiden with whom he is even supposed to be seriously in love. No commentator, with whom I am familiar, seems to have noticed one significant element in these disgusting utterances. They do vindicate Ophelia. They show that she had not "yielded all." Perhaps they thus serve the purpose which Shakspeare intended when he permitted himself to record them.

Henry Austin Clapp, a sympathetic student of Shakspeare, admitted that some of Ophelia's insane warblings were of a nature to arouse the question whether Hamlet had seduced her. Mr. Clapp did not think the dramatist intended to convey that meaning,—but he held that the suggestion was that Ophelia felt that she had suffered a spiritual sort of seduction. My own thought is, as I have stated in my romance,—namely, that Ophelia had helplessly endured an attack upon her soul.

Ophelia's songs can be easily explained in some such way as Mrs. Jameson accounts for them. She may be supposed to have heard many love songs of many sorts, just as modern girls have read such. Lines and stanzas had lodged in her memory, as passages of verse have fixed themselves like germs in the minds of readers. Delirium let them loose, just as delirium and senility have played similar tricks on other human beings.

Ophelia was, of course, love-crazed in a sense— and no discredit to her that she was! Most of her songs are as pure as snow and as lovely as wild, white lilies.

Hazlitt says, "Ophelia is a character almost too exquisitely touching to be dwelt upon. * * * Her love, her madness, her death are described with truest touches of tenderness and pathos." Hazlitt is right, so far as he goes, but he fails to suggest the strength of Ophelia's moral constitution, and the extent of her capacity for personal devotion to duty or to love, to either which she might be called upon to

consecrate the effort of her life—until the springs of
that life should be broken. The sweet bells of her
reason are not much jangled out of tune, even by
mania.

The commonly accepted opinion, that Gertrude
had been a faithless wife to her first husband, is
based entirely on ghostly testimony. That testimony, moreover, is not quite that of explicit assertion. Hamlet, with unfilial eagerness, believes the
Ghost's insinuations against his mother. Horatio
says nothing on the subject, but does not contradict
the Prince or argue with him about it. Nobody else
in the play manifests any suspicion by either word or
gesture. The world has either been silent like Horatio or has followed the son's example.

I suggest the propriety of studying Shakspeare's
general use of the supernatural element in order to
determine the function which it is most likely he intended to assign to it in the tragedy of Hamlet.

I have heard it seriously stated that the Ghost being disembodied spirit may be presumed to know
the facts in Gertrude's past life. How is the phantom presumed to learn facts which he did not know
when he was a man in the flesh? Is it to be supposed that death opens of itself the doors of history
to one who has died and reveals the interior of the

past? That is a large supposition. Is it supposed that as a spectral wanderer on the earth, this particular Ghost learned of the secret adultery by overhearing mundane whispers in the Danish court? The play provides no such whispers for him to overhear. Claudius murmurs, mutters and prays confession of the murder, and it may be fairly concluded that he had done so, in the period anterior to the opening of the play, and that an unseen haunting Presence overheard. Neither Claudius nor Gertrude ever confess adultery. Did they do so before the play begins and thus inform the Ghost of their past actions? Is it to be supposed that Shakspeare intended the audience and the reader to imagine utterances after the beginning of the play which they do not hear or read, but of which the Ghost knows? These are large suppositions as to Shakspeare's intentions. Is it to be supposed that some demon who had supernaturally acquired prior knowledge that Gertrude was guilty, was permitted or instructed to inform the kingly Ghost of it? That is a peculiar supposition as to infernal or supernal methods of dealing with the disembodied spirits of mortal men.

Did Shakspeare consciously base his representation of the Ghost's mental attitude on either one of the above suppositions? I am sure of only one thing,—and that is that I do not know the extent of the conscious purpose with which Shakspeare worked. But I have never taken stock in the notion that he was an inspired idiot, who did not know a good deal about what he was doing and why he did it. He was, at any rate, a dramatist, and it is fair to assume that what he felt unable to present with dramatic effect, he did not try to present at all.

As to other Shakspearean apparitions,—Banquo's Ghost speaks no word, and his appearance to Macbeth may therefore be construed in two ways. He may be understood as an outward and theatrically necessary representation to the audience of the thought in the murderer's own mind; or his appearance may be interpreted as an indication of some belief or fancy that the spirit of a murdered person was endowed with an especial power of showing itself to the murderer. Lady Macbeth and the guests at the banquet do not see the silent spectre to whom Macbeth speaks.

The Ghosts in "Richard III" are plainly intended for the edification of the audience. They are merely personifications of Richard's dreams. He does not himself see them. They are shown to the audience simply to let it know what Richard is dreaming

about. They speak for the benefit of the audience.
The Ghost of Julius Caesar, shown to Brutus, tells
nothing which Brutus did not previously know of the
past. Of the future, he says only, "Thou shalt see
me at Philippi."

The Ghost in "Hamlet" plays a different rôle from
any of these others, and one which does suggest an
intention on the part of the author to endow him with
something more like human individuality than that
with which the rest are equipped.

This Ghost does not appear to any person whom
It thinks had really or possibly injured him on earth.
He is made visible to four people who are all innocent of his death, Hamlet, Horatio, Marcellus and
Bernardo. He is never revealed to the vision of
Claudius, the actual murderer. He speaks directly
only to Hamlet. The text leaves it a little doubtful
whether or not the other three men do hear his command to "swear." Hamlet hears it. This is spoken
from underground, after he has left Hamlet on the
parapet. Since the voice comes upward, it is plau-
sible to suppose that the ghostly speaker is on his return journey to the Infernal regions. He has already spoken of the "foul crimes" he has himself
committed and the indescribable tortures to which he

is condemned. From the realm of punishment he comes, urging revenge, and then down again he goes into the empire of horror.

He speaks to Hamlet again in the presence of Gertrude, but she does not hear him.

He knows that Claudius had killed his earthly life and how, facts which the manner of his death makes it unlikely that he learned just at the time or immediately after the poison was poured into the "porches" of his sleeping ears. *But,* having been for some time now a spectral night walker on earth he could easily have learned, from the lonely midnight mutterings by Claudius to himself, who it was that had murdered him and how it was done. Similar processes of spiritual eavesdropping upon mortal men would reveal to him the reports sent abroad which implicated a snake in his death. In the same way, he might have learned of Gertrude's marriage. Mark this element in the case, the mock play represents the murder as performed in the way that the Ghost said it was, but it does not represent adultery at all.

Shakspeare has drawn more than one husband who, on more or less evidence, suspects a faithful wife of infidelity. I find no reason in any of his writings for basing a belief in Gertrude's guilt on the mere assumption that the dramatist intended a representation of ghostly infallibility.

I have worked out my romance therefore on what seems to me a reasonable theory; namely, that Shakspeare, in choosing his subject, was somewhat influenced by the dramatic possibilities involved in the dispute of his period about the rightfulness of marriage between a man and his brother's widow, and also by the emotional elements which the murder of the first by the second husband added to the theme. And finally, to all the other passions engendered by the situation, Shakspeare added the "towering" one of letting his Ghost develop a posthumous but unfounded suspicion and jealousy.

In this connection, I would call the reader's attention, as I have done in the romance itself, to the fact that it is not a wholly ignoble love which Claudius describes himself as feeling for Gertrude. Shakspeare does indeed place this woman, this incarnation of motherhood, amid tragical circumstances. He throws around her a tissue of false conjectures. He permits the men who should have known better to misunderstand her. But he makes it evident that she had not yielded to a brutal love or

Gertrude of Demark

even been ever subjected to the indignity of its approach to her.   Claudius says:

> "For myself—
> My virtue or my plague be it either which—
> She's so conjunctive to my life and soul,
> That as the star moves but in his sphere,
> I could not but by her."

INDEX

Index

hypocrisy, fears H plots his death, "my soul is sick," sees H, in soliloquy admits his plan to have H put to death in England 147-149, always blunders when frightened, critical commentary, on his character, "one shapeless, shadeless smirch of blackness" 149-152; 153, 154, 157, unsuspected of murder of K H 158, gentle with O 163-165, tells troubles to G 165-166, riot, Laertes enters, C's courage 167-169; 170, 171, 172, with Laertes, in G's dream 174, infuriates Laertes against H, moral rot from aestheticism 175-177, learns of H's return to Denmark, plans fencing contest 178-179; 180, 181, 182, arranges O's funeral service, thoughts in G's room while she sings, hysterics 184-190, enters grave yard 192; 194, 199, 200, ends ceremony at O's grave 203, progress towards crime 204, order for H's death found by H 205, "this canker of our nature" 208, plans method of poisoning H 209; 211, fencing scene, holds poison, shivers 214-215; 217, "Gertrude do not

[254]

drink" but does not snatch the cup 218, "part them they are incensed," "she faints to see them bleed," is stabbed, last articulate words he hears 219-221. Epilogue 221, 226; Appendix.

Coleridge, 26

Diaphantus, 82
Dignitary of the Church, 184

Fortinbras (the elder), 26, 27, 79
Fortinbras (the younger), 20, 27, 66

Gertrude, Queen, as Phantom 1-6, girlhood, marriage, friendly regard for C, speaks as Phantom, madonna-like motherhood, widowhood, anxiety about H, despair, hatred of convent life, long silence, betrothal to C, thanks Mother of God, kisses the wall 7-22, marries C, number of G's speeches in play, relations with C 23-28, begs H to leave off mourning and to stay in Elsinore, reference to time since K H's death 28-35, Ghost refers to G 51-53; 56, consultation about H 62-70; 78, why C influenced G 75-76, scene

Index

with O 76-80, pleads with C for H 90, Meeting with O 91-92; 93, at the play 95-101, effect of play 104-105, C's thought of G 107-109, C's words prove G's innocence 113-115; 119; 121, 122, 123, midnight interview with H, misunderstandings, does not see the Ghost, her love triumphant 124-143, a memory of H's childhood 144-145, tells C 146-149; 151; 152, 154, dreams 154-158, tender to C 158-159, O seeks and sees G 160-165, Laertes and riot 166-169, flower scene with O 169-172, compares O's sorrow with her own, dream, fear that her marriage was wrong passes 173-175, love for her son, C's love for her 176-177; 178, O's death 179-182, determines to vindicate O 182-183; 184, sings to C 185-189, grave yard scene 192-203, H at home 204, H's word and attitude toward G 206-208, Osric and the Queen 211-213, the fencing scene, her joy, her love, her death 214-220, Epilogue 222, 225, 226, Appendix.

Gertrude's brother, 7

Gertrude's father, 7

Ghost of King Hamlet (The Ghost), 36, 48-57; 69, 73, 93, 97, 102; 106; 115; 118; appears in G's room 138-142; 151; 207; 221, Appendix. *See* King Hamlet.

Goody (Hamlet's nurse), 16

Grave diggers, 192, 193, 197

Guildenstern, 63, 64, 71, 72, 73, 79, 80, 82, 106, 109, 110, 111, 112, 113, 122, 146, 149, 191, 205, 208

Hamlet, King, 5, half paternal half lover-like 7, 8, laughs at C 9, jealous of baby H 10, 11, fearful for G 13, 17, 18, 19, his blessing 20; 21, 22, "the dead king's love" 23, less a lover-husband than C 24,4 25, duel with Fortinbras day H was born 26, H's mourning for him 28-29; 30, 32, lapse of time since his death 33, 34, 35, 36, 38, appears as Ghost 49-55; 65, 67, H affected by K H's death 68, play given to represent his death 73-74, kisses G 78, inconsiderate of G 79, 95, 96, 99, 101, 108, C had not possessed G during K H's life time 114, "my father died in sin" 116, contrasted with C, H remembers how they teased C 117-

Index

118; 119, occasional mention 126-130, G's tender memory of him 131, relation to G 132-142; 148, 152, in G's dreams 155, 157, 158, G must mourn in secret for him 173, 174, H like K H 187; 204, signet ring used in a forgery 205, Appendix.

Hamlet, Prince, 2, 4, 9, birth, hated and loved by C 10-11, future, reminiscences of his childhood, 13-15; 16, attitude toward G 17-18, his toy 19; 20, 21, 22, fifty four of G's speeches concern H 24, K H kills Fortinbras on day of H's birth 26-27, wears black 27-28, offer of sonship by C 28-31, soliloquizes about G's marriage, misunderstands her intentions and character 32-34, interview with Horatio and officers 34-36, relation with O 37-47, interview on ramparts with Horatio, officers and Ghost 48-55, effect on H's mind 55-58, "antic disposition," O's love, intrusion in O's closet, discussed by Polonius and O 59-62, discussed by G, C, Polonius, Rosencranz and Guildenstern 63-70, interview with Polonius, Rosen-

[256]

cranz, Guildenstern and players 72-73, soliloquy, decides to have play acted 73-74; 76, 77, G's thoughts and memories of H 78-80, soliloquy in lobby, sees O, denies his love for her, calls her father a fool, bids her marry a fool or go to a nunnery 81-88, O's thought of H 89, C does not believe in H's love 89-90; 91, 92, theater scene, feeling for Horatio, reclines at O's feet, watches C and G, comments on play, makes insulting speeches to O, "what frighted with false fire!" 93-105, talks wildly, promises to see G 106-107; 108, 109, 110, 111, 112, 115, comes with drawn sword, sees C kneeling, remembers that in childhood his father and he teased C, hates but will not kill C while praying lest he go to heaven 116-120, "now could I drink hot blood," will not kill G 122-123, midnight interview with G, kills Polonius, half accuses G of complicity in murder of K H convinced she had no part, infuriated speech about her marriage not quite accusing her of adultery, compares

Index

C with K H, accuses C of having stolen the crown, s'ees and hears Ghost, a little softened, tells G he is not insane and is to go to England, drags out the body of Polonius 124-144, remembered as a child by G 144-145; 146, 147, 148, interview with C 149-150; 151, 153, flippant speeches 154; 155; 156, 157, 158, 161; 165, 173, 174, 175; G's love for H testified to by C 176; 178; O's aunt tells G that Laertes and Polonius loved H; G will not believe H guilty towards O 182-183; 187, H's childhood remembered by C 188; 189; with Horatio, grave yard scene, "what the fair Ophelia!" leaps into the grave, struggle with Laertes, goes 192-203; 204, tells Horatio of forging death warrant for Rosen'cranz and Guildenstern, calls G an evil name, sorry about Laertes, questions whether it would not be right to kill C now 205-209, accepts challenge to fence with Laertes, manner to Osric, 211-212; 213, fencing scene, claims to have been insane when he killed Polonius, kisses his hand to G, fences, refuses to drink, pricked by Laertes, weapons become changed, stabs Laertes, contest stopped, G thinks he is near her as she dies, stabs C 214-221, Epilogue—analysis of H's character, Laertes and H forgive each other, H's egoism at the last 221-227, Appendix.

Hecuba, 2, 72, 140

Horatio, 2, 34, 35, 48, 49, 50, 57, 93, 95, 106, 160, 161, 165, 191, 192, 195, 203, 204, 205, 207, 208, 211, 212, 219, 224, 225, Appendix.

Knight, 28

Laertes, 27, 37, 39—42, 47, 48, 157, 166, 167, 168, 169, 172 —176, 178—183, 185, 186, 192—204, 208—211, 213, 215, 216—219, 221, 223, 224, 226, Appendix.

Macbeth and Lady Macbeth, 6, Appendix.

Marcellus, 34, 36, 48, 57, Appendix.

Moberley, Rev. C. E., 110, 111, 112, Appendix.

"Old Norway," 14, 18, 20, 26, 27, 66

Index

Ophelia, 4, letter from H 17, cries shame to court ladies 18, mentioned by Phantom 37-39, scene with Laertes and Polonius, her courage, rightmindedness, counsels Laertes, defends H, "I shall obey, my lord" 39-45, lives in shadow of love and prayer 45-47, sees and loves H from afar, not tempted to disobey Polonius, reports H's intrusion into her closet, accepts idea C be told, 59-62; 67, 69, 70, 71, 72, scene with G 76-79, "Madam I wish it may" 80, scene in lobby "I was the more deceived," "Oh, heavenly powers restore him," soliloquy 81-89; 91, 92, 93, 95, 96, 97, H's words to O 102-104; 105, 126, 128, 129, 142, 149, learns of her father's death 152-154, illness 157; 158, O, insane, sings and tries to explain her song 160-165; 166, distributes flowers 169-171, her thought understood by G 173-174, death 179-183, suicide? 183-185; 186, 191, "maimed funeral rites," "but for great command" would have been buried in unconsecrated ground, tribute from G, Laertes grief and struggle with H 192-203; 207, 210, 214, 216. Epilogue 222, 223, Appendix.

Ophelia's aunt, 15, 16, 157, 182, 183

Ophelia's mother, 47

Osric, 211, 212, 213, 214, 219, 220, Appendix.

Pickwick, Samuel, 112

Players, 72-74, 93, 96-105, 213

Polack, the, 66

Polonius, 14, 27, 41, 42, 43, 44, 45, 46, 47, 60, 61, 62, 64, 65, 66, 67, 69, 70, 71, 72, 73, 79, 80, 81, 89, 91, 95, 105, 108, 109, 113, 122, 124, 125, 127, 144, 146, 147, 148, 149, 153, 158, 165, 175, 183, 210, 216, 223, Appendix.

Romeo and Juliet, 6

Rosencranz, 62, 63, 64, 71, 72, 73, 79, 80, 82, 106, 109, 110, 111, 112, 113, 122, 146, 149, 191, 205, 208. Appendix.

Scoloker, 82

Terry, Ellen, preface.

INDEX OF APPENDIX

Index of Appendix